S0-BOI-493

CHARLENE

I saw her first at a charity fund-raising dinner. She had recently given a large grant and she smilingly nodded when her name was called. I kept glancing at her as she conversed with the people next to her. The man on her right was in his thirties, an executive in a local hospital corporation; the woman on her left was in her sixties and talked plenty. She had a genuine interest in those people, and she made them feel it. She galvanized their attention.

Some instinct told me to find out more about her. I wanted to know why she seemed so happy. What was the source of her radiant impact? I had no idea in interviewing her that she would become my first miracle story . . .

Other Avon Books by
Don Fearheiley

ANGELS AMONG US

Avon Books are available at special quantity discounts for bulk purchases for sales promotions, premiums, fund raising or educational use. Special books, or book excerpts, can also be created to fit specific needs.

For details write or telephone the office of the Director of Special Markets, Avon Books, Dept. FP, 1350 Avenue of the Americas, New York, New York 10019, 1-800-238-0658.

MIRACLES

DON FEARHEILEY

AVON BOOKS ◆ NEW YORK

If you purchased this book without a cover, you should be aware that this book is stolen property. It was reported as "unsold and destroyed" to the publisher, and neither the author nor the publisher has received any payment for this "stripped book."

MIRACLES is an original publication of Avon Books. This work has never before appeared in book form.

AVON BOOKS
A division of
The Hearst Corporation
1350 Avenue of the Americas
New York, New York 10019

Copyright © 1994 by Don Fearheiley
Published by arrangement with the author
Library of Congress Catalog Card Number: 94-94319
ISBN: 0-380-77652-9

All rights reserved, which includes the right to reproduce this book or portions thereof in any form whatsoever except as provided by the U.S. Copyright Law. For information address Avon Books.

First Avon Books Printing: November 1994

AVON TRADEMARK REG. U.S. PAT. OFF. AND IN OTHER COUNTRIES, MARCA REGISTRADA, HECHO EN U.S.A.

Printed in the U.S.A.

RA 10 9 8 7 6 5 4 3 2 1

Dedicated
to
LUCI
Cherished daughter and forever a miracle

*None of you will ever believe
unless you see miracles.*

—John 4:48

*All change is a miracle to contemplate;
but it is a miracle which is taking place every instant.*

—Thoreau

*In a time of change you have to have
miracles. And miracles do happen.*

—President Bill Clinton

CONTENTS

FOREWORD

When Carter Means called Jim Bailey into his office Jim felt a little on edge, like a factory line boss facing new ownership that wanted to downsize. Not that Jim really needed to worry about his job. Carter had made it plain when he hired Jim, ". . . we'll make religion front page."

Being religion editor for a metropolitan newspaper isn't bad for someone only a few years out of college. But religion was not Jim's beat at the small daily where he worked in southern Iowa. A sports reporter with his own column, "Bailey's Banter," and proud of it, honoring Grantland Rice as his spiritual ancestor and figuring he'd need ten years of experience before even thinking of moving to a major city and landing a sports column.

But the thing was—Jim's Iowa daily was part of a chain that also owned the paper where Carter Means reigned as managing editor. And Carter had seen an article Jim wrote about the spiritual leanings of the local basketball coach. Prayer in the locker room before and after each game. Flavoring pep talks with Bible quotations. Emphasizing that how the game is played is more important than winning or losing. Allowing no profane language in the heat of battle, or in practice, or in the shower, or anywhere else within the coach's earshot.

A most unusual coach, and Jim had been able to profile him in depth—describing his childhood upbringing by his grandmother after his parents were killed, the rededication of his life to God during the Korean War when he and the Second Division fought their way out of the Chinese ambush at Kunu-ri, the fairness and honesty that infused his coaching, and the impact his character had on his players long after they graduated from high school.

And Carter had read a later article—when Jim described the effect of a player's death. He had collapsed on the court during a game with no warning of any heart problems. But he had been the heart of his team—a star forward—greatly admired by everyone who knew him. Jim profiled reactions, and covered the emotional and moving remarks of the coach and various players during the funeral.

"I've got more sports reporters than I need," Carter told Jim during that first interview. "And piles of applicants for any opening that might come up. But who wants to write about religion?" He stared at Jim quizzically.

Not me, Jim thought, but what he said was, "I imagine you have a lot of applicants for that job, too."

"Right." Carter gestured to a pile of folders on his desk. "But those applicants don't give me what I want. Do you know what I want?"

Jim shook his head.

"A lack of experience."

Jim's mouth fell open. Carter smiled thinly. "Not a lack of writing experience," he said, "a lack of *reli-*

gion writing experience. All these applicants are experienced journalists, but their whole background has been religion. I want someone who approaches religion from a totally fresh viewpoint, someone who can write about religion as about Kentucky trailing UCLA by two points with ten seconds to go. But someone"—Carter smiled wryly—"who can still write with sensitivity and sympathy and understanding. I think Jim Bailey might be able to do that. Your pieces on the old coach and the player who died on the floor had heart, a sense of empathy far deeper than simply reporting facts."

Jim sat quietly, staring at Carter staring at him. Finally Carter added, "What often passes for religion writing is listing church activities or passing along puff pieces sent out by institutional public relations departments. I want to make our readers feel that religion is something more important than that."

Jim felt he had to be careful in what he said, and tried to ease again into his long-held ambition to be a sports columnist, but Carter only shook his head. "You're years away from writing a sports column for a paper this size, but you could go to the head of the line if you wanted to try this new field."

Then Carter smiled. "My religion editor was seventy-two when he retired. I want someone young, who can look at religion with fresh eyes, who has the guts even to get controversial when that's needed. I want someone who can come up with fresh angles. Religion has been with us a long time, but what are the current issues? How is religion relevant in modern life?"

Jim didn't know what to say, and Carter went on. "As I see it, Jim, you've got quite a decision. You can stay with sports, pay your dues, and spend several more years with a smaller paper, or you can go to work for me right now—as religion editor. And look, let's make it easier—maybe you won't like what you do. Maybe *I* won't like what you do. So let's consider it a test. If it doesn't work out here you can go back to your old job in sports at your present paper or maybe another paper in our chain. You won't be penalized in job or salary."

All Jim could say was, "I don't know."

"Take your time to decide. But understand this"— his expression grew serious—"I think you can do the job, and I'll support you all the way. You come up with the ideas, and we'll make religion front page."

After a lot of thought and soul-searching, Jim did accept the challenge, and in the first year on the job he had hit front page a number of times—not always to the delight of the religious community. Religious people were human like everyone else—even pastors and priests were human. And when they erred, human interest decreed somber headlines. But Jim seized on positive elements as well, running a series of interviews with people who claimed angels had helped them overcome obstacles or escape tragedy. The first article in that series made the front page. Another front-page story related how a group of churches was ministering to the homeless during cold winter nights.

So after one year Jim was satisfied with his progress as religion editor. And Carter seemed satisfied. True to his word, Jim was given freedom to come up with ideas and support for getting them prominently exposed. In fact, Jim had sensed a growing antagonism from some of the staffers who felt he was getting preferential treatment. Not that this matter was crucial, but it did serve to put an edge on what appeared to be Jim's close relationship to the boss.

Jim certainly looked up to Carter and viewed him as a mentor. But Jim always became a little unsettled when Carter called him into his office for a private conversation. Was he unhappy, dissatisfied, critical of what Jim had done or hadn't done? Carter was a hands-on editor, conferring with many people, settling down in front of a staffer's desk when he had something to say. The times when he went one-on-one in his own office usually marked a special problem or request.

Carter came right to the point. "Jim, I've got an idea for a series of articles."

Jim waited him out.

"Miracles," Carter said.

Jim's brain locked, and Carter continued. "Miracles—miracles today. Everyday miracles. Miracles happening all around us, but we don't see them. Modern-day miracles, the greatest evidence of God at work. Talk about human interest—some of it could be front page."

Jim's mind raced to the Bible. Moses and the plagues? Joshua at Jericho? Jesus walking on water? Those kind of miracles?

"I'm not sure I understand," Jim said.

"What do people think when they hear the word 'miracle'? Something dramatic in the Bible. Something that seems impossible. But if God really exists, if he is still active in the world today, then he's still performing miracles. But we may not recognize them, because they may seem like small and everyday stuff. Let's make people recognize them."

Jim hesitated, careful of what to say. "You mean—

the kind of miracles preachers talk about in their Sunday morning sermons?"

"Forget preaching," Carter said firmly. "Don't think about those Bible miracles. Find me people, flesh and bone, common, everyday people—time-card-punching, grocery-shopping, carpooling-kids-to-school people who have experienced miracles in their lives. Write about the kind of miracles we can understand, and we may put them on the front page. Hey, look," Carter said, seeing Jim hesitate, "I know we won't be able to use all the material you collect, not in the newspaper. But we'll be able to use some of the stories you find. Think you can do it?"

My mentor, my coach, Jim thought, looking at me and talking like the team needed motivating at halftime. Think I can do it? Can I win? Can I find miracle stories? Yes, Coach, yes!

But all Jim said was, "I'll give it a try."

But after he got involved in the project, he realized that most of his stories could not properly appear in a daily newspaper. But they could be brought together in the form of a book.

This book . . .

CHARLENE'S HAT

I saw her first at a charity fund-raising dinner for the Fred Wallace Speech and Hearing Center. Normally, Edith Fillmore would have covered this event, but she was in New York with a package theater tour the paper sponsored twice a year. And since the major speaker was going to be Dr. Alfred Manning, a well-known Presbyterian pastor, I got the assignment. On this night Dr. Manning voiced glowing words for a universally admired program that reached out to the hearing impaired without regard to race or religion or the family's ability to pay.

But what absorbed more of my attention was the middle-aged woman seated near the center of the head table. She had been introduced as Charlene Porter, who recently gave a large grant to the Fred Wallace Center. She smilingly nodded to the audience when her name was called. Her smile was attractive, but I noticed the hat first. No one else wore one—at the head table or in the room. A blue hat, with a narrow brim curling up. A character?—my first thought. But then I kept glancing at her as she conversed with the persons next to her.

The man on her right was in his thirties, an executive in a local hospital corporation who seemed to drink a lot of iced tea. The woman on her left was in her sixties. She barely touched her iced tea, but she talked plenty. So did the executive, because the woman in the hat galvanized their attention.

She was animated—yes. But she had another quality, unseen, but as real as gravity surrounding mass. Empathy. I could spot it from as far away as my table. She had a genuine interest in those people—disparate as they were—and she made them feel it.

I wanted to know more about her, and determined to call for an interview, using her gift to the center as an excuse. I had no idea whether interviewing her would generate a story. Some instinct told me to find out more about her. I wanted to know why she seemed so happy. What was the source of her radiant impact? And why, why that blue hat with the curling brim?

She became my first miracle story . . .

Daisy's hackles rose, but Charlene didn't notice. She was staring at the Carrington vase her husband had given her on their thirteenth wedding anniversary. That had been a rough year. Ken almost lost his business that year when he couldn't make payments on a loan, and their daughter Rachel died.

Tears scalded Charlene's eyes. She'd been thinking a lot about Rachel lately. Rachel, with her spindly legs, her blond, curly hair bouncing above deep-set blue eyes and lips that met the world with a smile—a silent smile. She was almost totally deaf. But she could make a sound when she laughed, and Ken had given her a nickname—"Gigglelips." Always a happy child, she especially liked the times she spent at the Fred Wallace Center as she related to other hearing-impaired children as well as the hearing children who were brought in for a balanced group experience. But one time Rachel didn't giggle—when she was running through the house chasing a ball and knocked over the vase that stood where the Carrington now was placed. Charlene remembered Rachel's heartbroken stare. And all of a sudden Charlene's most pressing need was to make her handicapped little five-year-old daughter feel better, using sign and a reassuring hug.

Then one year later in a hospital room it was Rachel who tried to make her mother feel better. Rachel, still smiling and signing to show her love despite some kind of brain tumor the doctor called glioblastoma multiforme. Until the end she was a Gigglelips.

After Rachel's death Charlene experienced extreme mood swings, abruptly crying and then sitting for long periods without any focus on what happened around her. She went into therapy for depression, and eventually found a sense of peace. She was grateful she still had her other children, Gina and Jeff, and of course, Ken. Her husband had been her strength throughout the ordeal with Rachel, and then during her own ordeal of fighting depression. He had always been there for her, even before they were married, when she fought with her parents who said he was too old for her, that twenty years was too big a difference, and she shouldn't even think about getting serious with the man who employed her. But keeping

his books taught her a lot about that man, and every
day she learned more about his honesty and character. He said they made a good team, and as time
passed she knew their teamwork could extend far beyond the walls of their auto supply company.

Now she heard a deep rumble of low-pitched
sound. Daisy's head was raised as she stared at the
door. Charlene could hear nothing, but she knew the
men had probably arrived, pulling up in the driveway.
She wished she hadn't made this appointment. She
didn't want this meeting. She didn't want to see anybody, but Ed had prevailed. At least talk to them, he
said. A sweet boy, her son-in-law, but too interested
in money. Maybe all bankers were. But he made Gina
happy.

All of a sudden Daisy's bark erupted just before
the doorbell rang. Wilma came hurrying from the
kitchen to open the door.

"Daisy sit," Charlene said, as Daisy let out another
bark. Charlene was used to the terrifying timbre of
Daisy's bark, but most of her visitors were not. She
always enjoyed their demeanor when facing for the
first time the broad jaw and solid, muscular body of
a sixty-seven-pound pit bull, pound for pound the
world's strongest breed of dog. And Daisy was a
good representative—prettier than most—a tan brin-
dle with white feet. But she was also well trained and
would only attack when facing a threat. Ken had
raised her from a seven-week-old puppy.

Charlene stood as Wilma invited the two men to
enter, one carrying a large black portfolio.

"Mrs. Porter," the first man took the lead in smiling, as Charlene extended her hand.

"Good morning, Mr. Speers."

"And you remember Mr. Layhew?"

"Yes, indeed," she said, shaking the other man's hand. "Please sit down."

After they were settled she asked, "Would you like some tea or coffee?"

Mr. Speers nodded, "Coffee would be nice."

"Coffee," echoed Mr. Layhew. Charlene smiled at Wilma, who left the room.

The three were silent a moment, then Mr. Layhew cleared his throat. "That's a nice-looking dog."

"Daisy is one of the family," Charlene said. "She doesn't know she's a dog."

"What kind of dog is it?" Mr. Layhew asked.

"American Pit Bull Terrier."

His smile was uncertain. "A beautiful dog."

"Thank you," Charlene said. More silence.

"I'm sorry Ed couldn't be here," Mr. Speers said. "We could have come another time."

"No need for that," she smiled, "my son-in-law is already on your side." Just as my son is, she thought. She didn't tell them that Jeff wanted to be here, too, but he was upstairs sleeping after his late night out.

Mr. Layhew nodded. "I'm still sorry Ed was called out of town."

"Even bankers have to travel sometimes."

At that moment Wilma entered with a tray and three cups of coffee. Mr. Speers poured in cream and carefully dropped in one lump of sugar before settling back, stirring the coffee. Mr. Layhew took it black, as did Charlene. Wilma left the room.

Mr. Speers sipped his coffee. "I was telling Mr. Layhew that this house was built around the turn of the century."

"In 1908," Charlene said. "My husband was the fifth owner."

"A lot of changes have taken place in the neighborhood since then."

"And you represent one of the biggest changes," Charlene said.

Mr. Layhew grinned. "We hope a change for the better." Charlene smiled without saying anything.

Mr. Speers cleared his throat. "We've been able to obtain all the property Mr. Layhew wants for the Crestfield Heights development."

"Except mine?" Charlene smiled. Mr. Speers smiled in return.

"Your four acres would cap it off."

"Mrs. Porter," Mr. Layhew set his cup on the table in front of him, "you're aware that Crestfield Heights will offer five hundred condos and two hundred offices—landscaped with trees, ponds, shrubbery, walking paths, and fountains to make a unique working and living environment for this city. We'd like to include your property."

"Sitting at the intersection of Oakmont and Twenty-first puts you in a strategic location," Mr. Speers added.

"I understand that."

"Your son-in-law tells me that you were already considering moving," Mr. Speers said.

Charlene nodded. "The house is too big now. And with Ken gone—" Her voice fell off and Mr. Layhew opened his portfolio.

"I brought some drawings that render the area near the intersection."

The first drawing showed an elaborate stone entrance to a shaded boulevard with buildings in the background fronting a huge fountain. "This entrance would be approximately where your property is." Mr. Layhew showed another drawing, depicting a scene from the residential area. And a third drawing, featuring business offices surrounded by a parking area.

"I'm sure your development will be beautiful," Charlene said. "I'm just not ready to sell."

The men sat quietly. Mr. Layhew put the drawings back into the portfolio. "I know this has been a difficult time for you, Mrs. Porter. We've certainly enjoyed our previous visits with you, and the discussions with your lawyer, but we did want to spend this additional time informally with you to see if you have any further questions."

"I believe not."

"If our offer isn't satisfactory—"

"Your offer seems generous."

Both men stood. "We are facing a deadline," Mr. Layhew said. "I hope you can come to a decision soon."

Charlene extended her hand. "Thanks for coming by. And we will let you know." Charlene walked with them to the door, Daisy following at her heels.

Mr. Layhew smiled again. "You know, we could build you a beautiful place in Crestfield Heights."

"We'll be talking to you, Mr. Layhew." She watched the men walk to the car and pull away.

In the car Mr. Layhew spoke. "I don't think we accomplished a thing."

"Her son-in-law and daughter are with us. She'll come around."

"You think she's holding us up for more money?"

"No."

"I don't like the way she acted. Like she had no interest in our offer."

Mr. Speers shrugged. "She's still grieving over her husband."

* * *

Charlene slowly closed the door. Why did she feel so tired? A moment of dread gripped her. She remembered how it had felt years before, when the world almost drowned her in an ocean of depression. Was she going to go through it again, the tasteless days of emptiness when nothing seemed worth doing? When life itself seemed a burden without relief? She would fight it. This time she wouldn't let the dragon seize her. But with Ken gone—what did it really matter? What did any of it matter anymore? Daisy licked at her hand.

She moved back to her chair. She liked feeling the green velvet fabric on the arm of the large club chair that supported her weight with plush softness. She rubbed her hand over the chair arm's fabric again and again, staring at her empty cup on the table. Wilma entered and started collecting the cups.

"Would you like more coffee?" she asked.

Charlene shook her head. "But leave my cup."

Wilma nodded. Charlene watched her leave and realized again how fortunate she was to have Wilma. She had come to them during the dark time when Charlene was wrestling with her demons after Rachel died. A woman newly widowed, without children, having lived on a farm all her life. Ken had wanted a woman who could live in and always be at hand, ready to help Charlene in any way. But over the years Wilma had become more than a companion; she was a close friend.

Now Charlene stared at the empty cup and saw her life. You drink, and then the cup is empty. You live, and then someone dies. And after everything that happens, what is left?

A daughter is left, married to a banker. A son is

left who has dropped out of school three times. And the house is left, but everyone wanted her to sell it.

Maybe she ought to make an appointment with Dr. Keller. He had made her feel better before. But no— she wasn't sick. Not this time. She wouldn't let herself be sick. She just missed Ken so much. Silly fool, she told herself. These were not the times to be so dependent on a man. No woman should unconsciously lean on a man, seeking his approval, waiting for his opinion to guide her own decisions, looking forward to his company, needing the fact of his existence for her happiness.

The cup before her was still empty.

Upstairs Jeff Porter lay on his bed staring at the ceiling. He had a lot to think about, especially after last night. Candice had broken up with him. She said she didn't want to keep seeing someone who was going nowhere. Which, ironically, was how his father had once described him. Jeff had tried to explain to his father that he just didn't like school. He didn't want to go to college. He wanted to go to work for the company. Since his father owned five auto parts outlets in the city and had opened branches in six other county-seat towns in southern Indiana, why couldn't he start working and learn the business from the ground up? But his father said a degree comes first. So Jeff went back to school a second time. Went a whole year at a local community college. Another no go. Now what had been the controlled explosion of an underground test became an atmospheric fireball when the report card came. The fallout of that confrontation made Jeff retreat to the same local college. Another wasted semester. What did algebra and lit and sociology have to do with anything that interested him? So Jeff wouldn't go to school and his father wouldn't give him a job. Stalemate. Jeff ended up taking odd jobs until he got hired by a concrete contractor.

Then came the final confrontation, only four months before his father's death. Mother had tried to be peacemaker, but this time she had little effect on his father. Things were said—words like "go to school or forget about any future help or support," words that built a wall of separation that made Jeff feel even more like an illegal alien.

But all that changed with his father's operation and the complications that developed after an aortic heart valve replacement. The doctors could not stabilize him. All the old arguments were forgotten, and Jeff and his father came together in a renewed recognition of their love for each other.

His father went into intensive care, and finally, the doctors allowed all the family members to see him. When Jeff had reached out to touch his father's hand he thought he saw a slight tremor in one finger, and a small movement in the lips that that made Jeff bend low to hear the words. Barely above a whisper, but he heard every word clearly. "You can work for me, my son."

After his father's death he was amazed at how he felt. Not at the grief and sadness, but something else. It seemed like most of his life he had resisted his father, resenting the arbitrary way his father tried to control his life. The years had seemed like a continuing struggle to find himself, to stand on his own, to be independent. But now something was missing, the external pressure pushing him in a given direction. His father's attitude had been a constant, and now it was gone. And somehow without it he felt lost, sometimes feeling he were sleepwalking through a fog.

But last night was a cold shower to wake him up. He liked Candice—a lot. Maybe more than that. He had nothing more to prove to his father, but he did have something to prove to Candice. He wanted to talk to her again. Tonight.

A tap on the door made him sit up. "Yes?"

"Jeff, I need to tell you something." Wilma's voice.

Jeff moved to the door and cracked it open. He was wearing shorts. "What is it, Wilma?"

"I'm sorry to bother you," she said, "but I'm worried about your mother."

"What's wrong?"

"She hasn't been feeling well."

"Is she sick?"

"She's been sitting in the chair for the last three hours, just staring at her cup."

"Just a minute." Jeff moved to his closet and grabbed a bathrobe. Then he opened the door.

"She doesn't respond when I say anything." Jeff could sense the fear in her voice. "She seemed all right when the men were here."

"Men?"

"Mr. Speers and that land developer for Crestfield Heights."

Jeff made a face. "I forgot they were coming."

"She talked to them and after they left she sat and just keeps rubbing the arm of the chair. She hasn't eaten and won't say anything."

He hurried from the room, Wilma following him down the stairs. When he saw his mother he noticed her hand still rubbing the arm. He touched her hand, but it kept moving.

"Mother?"

She ignored him, staring at the cup.

"Mother, can you hear me?"

Only the hand movement, the staring. He reached and picked up the cup. Her eyes followed. He handed the cup to Wilma. "How about taking it to the kitchen?"

Wilma left. Charlene's eyes followed her. Jeff moved directly in front of her. "Mother, look at me. Can you hear me?"

Slowly Charlene nodded.

"Are you feeling all right?"

Again Charlene nodded, and she leaned forward, trying to rise. Jeff held her arm as she slowly stood.

"Is something wrong?" he asked.

"Later," she said, moving away.

"Mother, let's talk—"

She shook her head. "I need to lie down awhile."

"Mother, please—" His voice trailed off as she left the room. He was worried. He had been ten years old when his mother had gone to live at Carehaven Acres for several months. He remembered going there with his father on weekly visits, and how his mother acted as though she barely knew them. And he remembered being afraid. He was afraid now. Should he call Gina? His sister was an alarmist. Don't call yet. The doctor, he could contact the doctor. Dr. Keller would be able to tell if Mother were going into depression again. But it was too early for panic. Mother was still in a normal grieving process. He'd wait until tomorrow, see how she was tomorrow.

Tomorrow . . .

Upstairs Charlene moved to her dressing table and stopped, staring into the mirror. Where had she been just now? At the bottom of a well where everything that was said was an echo from a long way off. Time had absented itself in the presence of a feeling dark and hopeless. Time was the touch of yesterday and today, but not tomorrow. No tomorrow was worthy of dreams.

She looked in the mirror and saw an old woman.

The bed was inviting. She sank onto it, and then didn't want to lie down. She didn't want the bed. She wanted the picture that stared at her from the far wall. She stood and moved toward it, counting the steps. She was always good at math. Seventeen steps. But she was more than seventeen in the picture. Twenty-two when she got married. Her parents disapproved. He's forty-two. He's too old, they told her. She told her parents—live with it.

She took the picture from the wall. She and Ken were leaving the church after the wedding reception. She was wearing her traveling outfit and hanging onto Ken's arm, smiling like a leprechaun finding a four-leaf clover. Had she really ever smiled like that? When was the last time she felt like smiling? Ken had made her smile. He could always make her smile—from the moment of this picture until the time he told her about the operation. She didn't smile after that.

She outlined his face with her finger, then traced along her own shape until she touched the outline of the hat. Ken had insisted she buy that hat when they saw it at Loveman's. She had been looking for a sweater, but he liked the hat perched on a nearby stand. A blue hat, with a narrow brim that curled up. He said it made her look like a child. She said she already looked young enough, but he only laughed.

She still had the hat, stored in the attic. She hadn't worn it in years. When the gray hair came she felt one relic ought to retire the other relic. Suddenly she wanted to find the hat and try it on, but even as she looked at the picture the desire faded. She rehung the picture and moved back to the bed. This time she lay down. Maybe tomorrow I'll look for the hat, she thought.

Tomorrow . . .

Jeff didn't feel confident on the drive to Candice's house. When he phoned her she said he could come after dinner, but the tone of her voice echoed the resonance of the blowup last night.

He had trouble believing it had happened. The fact is that he and Candice had hit it off from the first time he met her, at the Camelback Club when he had stopped in with Jed and Carl. She was at a table with three other women. All of them were wearing cowgirl hats with vests and boots. His favorite singer, Vince Gill, was mellow-bellowing out a song accompanied by linedancers crowding the dance floor.

Carl knew one of the girls and the next thing introductions were being made at the table. Jeff paired off with Candice and found out she was divorced, had a five-year-old daughter named Carol, and was three years older than he. She was a receptionist and billing clerk for the Physical Therapy Department of Baptist Hospital. Later the guys laughed about Jeff and his "old" woman. But inside Jeff was laughing the loudest—Candice was far more attractive than any other girl he saw that night.

The next day Jeff had phoned Candice and asked for a movie date. She accepted and they discovered they had a lot in common. They laughed a lot, liked the same kind of movies (romantic thrillers) and music (new country). And he found out he liked to work puzzles and read books to Carol. He often talked about his family, but while Candice sympathized with his frustrations at home, she showed little sympathy for his indifferent attitude about school. Still, she kept seeing him. Four months of what he thought was a growing relationship, and then came last night.

They had gone out to a family restaurant with Carol. Back home he had read Carol a Seuss book before bedtime. He noticed that Candice was looking at him with a strange expression. Then Carol insisted that Jeff tuck her in. He had done this before, but the prayer thing was different.

Carol asked Jeff to pray that they could be a real family and live together. Back in the living room Candice said they needed to talk. But she did most of the talking, her voice low so that Carol wouldn't hear. She said she liked him a lot. And on a physical level she had no complaints. But she didn't see a future for them. They'd better break it off.

Jeff asked why. Candice said Carol was growing too attached to him. He still didn't understand, so she told him no matter how much she liked him and enjoyed being with him, she was looking for more than a good dating partner and fun times. If she fell in love she'd be thinking of getting married again. But he wasn't ready for marriage, she said. He argued she should give their relationship more time. She reminded him that he had been spinning his wheels for four years since graduating from high school. He argued. She asked what he called playacting with books and dropping out of school three times, working at jobs where he had no intention of building a career. She said she didn't want to get serious with someone who seemed to be going nowhere.

That was last night. He was entering her neighborhood, a middle-class section where the streets were named after states. Her house was on the corner of Dakota and Maryland, a white clapboard with a small porch containing two red metal chairs. Candice's ex-husband paid alimony that helped her with the payments. Perry Robinson was a buyer in the Better Men's Clothing Department of Harper-Benning and he tried to see his daughter every weekend. Jeff had met him twice, a nice guy.

Pulling up in front of her house, Jeff turned off the lights. He had a lot to say to Candice, but he didn't know what effect it would have. He only knew he didn't want last night as the epitaph to their relationship.

He knocked on the front door, knowing the doorbell didn't work. Candice appeared, wearing a patterned pullover with splashes of light pink against a gray background that matched her gray pants. Her hair was tied in a ponytail.

"Come in." She wasn't smiling.

Inside he looked for Carol. Candice read his mind. "Carol's staying with Jillian McCall tonight."

"Jillian McCall—?"

"I've told you about her. She's Carol's deaf friend."

"Right. She goes to the Fred Wallace Center."

Candice nodded. "Tomorrow's the day Carol goes as one of the hearing children. Jillian's mother will take them both to the center in the morning." She motioned to a chair. "Sit down."

"How about your sitting and letting me stand?"

She nodded and moved to the couch.

"I thought we said everything we needed to last night," she said evenly.

He shook his head. "You said what *you* wanted."

"I don't see why anything else needs to be said."

"So why did you let me come back tonight?"

She was silent. Finally, she shrugged. "Nothing you say will make me change my mind."

"But you wanted to hear what I might say. Doesn't that tell you something?"

She still kept silent. He went on, "That may mean you haven't closed me out yet."

She shook her head. "I said I liked you. I enjoyed our dates. But I don't want Carol getting confused. It's time to move on."

"I'm going to move on," he said earnestly, sitting down on the couch beside her. "Listen—last night I did a lot of thinking. You were right about me, everything you said. I was always blaming Dad for where I was. But I know I'm the one responsible for everything I did or didn't do, and for wasting time these past four years. Dad told me before he died that I could work for him. I haven't done anything about that, but I will. I keep remembering all the arguments we had and wishing I could go back and change things. I can't change the past, but I can make a change for the future."

"You're going back to school?"

He shook his head. "Not full time. I'll pick up some business courses, but I'm finally going to start working at Car Tech. Gina and I are going to own that company someday, and eventually I hope to buy her out. And grow, I want us to grow. Maybe—" he smiled, "—become another AutoZone or Carquest."

She said nothing, and they stared at each other a long moment. "Well?" he asked.

"Well, what?"

"What do you think?"

"What am I supposed to think?"

"You can think we have a good thing going. Four months doesn't mean a lifetime, but it's long enough to be willing to give our relationship another chance."

She smiled and then her expression grew thoughtful. "There's still Carol—"

"She knows who her real father is."

"But you heard her prayer."

"Okay. She likes me. I'm glad. But aren't you going to have that problem with anyone you date regularly for a length of time?"

She slowly nodded. "I suppose so."

"Let's let it happen naturally—whatever happens. Between you and I, and between Carol and I." He focused on her eyes, brown eyes that seemed to get larger as she stared at him.

"Well?" she asked.

"Well, what?"

"What do you think?"

"What am I supposed to think?"

She smiled. "You can think that kissing me is not a bad idea."

He leaned forward. She was right. Definitely a good idea. "Can I see Carol tomorrow?" he asked.

"Sure."

"Who's going to pick her up at the center?"

"I'm supposed to get the girls after work, but my supervisor phoned right before you got here and asked me to work late tomorrow with some special billings. I was going to call Perry and see if he could get the girls and stay with them until I get home."

"What if I picked up the girls? Would Jillian's mother mind?"

"She'd be grateful. She's taking inventory at Wayfare's in the Hunter's Lane Mall, and her husband is

out of town. I was going to keep Jillian with me until
her mother could get off."

"Remember I told you how my sister used to go to
the Fred Wallace Center? I'll enjoy seeing the place
again."

"All right, I'll phone Mary and check that she feels
good about your picking up Jillian. If that's okay, she
can call the center that you'll be the one coming by
for them."

Charlene was still lying on the bed. She hadn't
been sleeping. Once Wilma had come to the door
asking about fixing something to eat. Charlene had
sent her away. She remembered how Rachel liked
eating cornbread crumbled into a glass, milk poured
over it, and sprinkled with sugar. Charlene had
learned that from her grandfather. She tried it with
two-year-old Rachel, who took to it like Daisy eating
a steak bone. Rachel would eat almost anything—
never finicky like Gina was. Thin, always thin—
looking like she was malnourished, but full of energy.
She had a habit of bouncing up on her father's lap
when he was reading the newspaper, energetically
signing so that any encroaching page soon ceased being wrinkle-free. She got by with that, and a whole
lot more than Ken would have allowed from any
other child. Ken once called Rachel their last great
gift from God. And then God took back the gift.
Charlene's lips tightened. Now God had Ken. But
surely—somewhere in God's Heaven—Ken was able
to hold a curly, blond-headed girl with spindly legs
on his lap and watch her eat cornbread soaked in
milk lightly sprinkled with sugar.

Slowly Charlene sat up, moving her legs off the
bed onto the floor. There was no place on earth she

wanted to be. But she was afraid if she stayed in bed
the dragon could reach her and drag her down to
where she had been once before. The well of depression was always near, but she must never even look
into it. That's how she fell last time, looking and losing her balance and falling. She would look upward,
climb upward—and she thought of the attic. She
would look for her blue hat with the curled brim—
her honeymoon hat.

Flipping the attic switch lit the huge room with
three incandescent lights that threw in harsh relief
against the walls the shadows of stacked boxes and
memorabilia. Charlene stumbled over a dumbbell left
over from Jeff's ambition to be Mr. Olympia. There,
in the far corner, stood the dress form she had used
to make her honeymoon traveling outfit—a blue suit
of a wool and silk blend—and many other garments
that had gone to Goodwill years ago. But her hat was
still here, somewhere.

She blew the dust from the top of a trunk near the
dress form. Jewelry—she had forgotten about all the
jewelry that Aunt Gertrude had left her. Loud, rau-
cous jewelry that matched the flamboyant personality
of an office manager for Penney's. Then she moved
to another nearby trunk.

Inside she saw the round hat box. She carefully un-
tied the cords that crossed on the top, and there it
was—the blue hat with the narrow brim curling up.
She slowly stood and placed the hat on her head. A
mirror, she needed a mirror. There was one up here.
Looking around she spotted it leaning against the
bricks of the chimney. She moved to it and stared,
thinking of the photograph hanging in her bedroom.
She had been smiling when she wore this hat so
many years ago. Happy. Looking with great anticipa-

tion to the future. Expecting great and wonderful things to happen. Holding the arm of a man who had chosen the hat and insisted they get it for her. The man was gone, but the blue hat remained. And as she adjusted the hat on her head, turning and twisting her head to get different perspectives, she knew his love would always be with her.

When Jeff arrived home from Candice's he was anxious to check on his mother. Tapping on the door, he was surprised to hear that voice so strong.

"Come in."

He opened the door and another surprise. Instead of being in bed, she was sitting at her dressing table looking at herself in the mirror.

"Are you all right?"

"You always ask me that," she said. "How do you like this?" She turned to face him, patting the blue hat on her head.

"Pretty," he said.

"You don't remember it, but your father picked this out for me. I wore it on our honeymoon."

"Sure. The picture."

"I feel better than I've felt in a long time. Wearing this hat, holding it, even just seeing it—reminds me of something I should never forget."

"I'm glad you feel better," he said.

"It's almost like a miracle, finding this hat."

"A couple of things I wanted to ask you about, Mother. First, I want to start working at Car Tech."

"Of course," she said, "the company will be yours one day."

"I'll take some courses. Not like Father wanted, but—"

She interrupted. "You're not your father. He did it his way. You do it yours."

He nodded, relieved. "I know Harry Woods does a good job running the company, and I like him a lot."

"He'll take care of you," she said. "He'll see that you learn what you need."

"The other thing, I'd like you to come with me to Chadway Park tomorrow afternoon."

"Why?"

"You know my—friend, Candice, has a five-year-old daughter, Carol, and Carol has a friend named Jillian who is partially deaf and goes to the Fred Wallace Center."

Charlene stiffened, and Jeff went hurriedly on. "Carol attends as one of the hearing children. So anyway, neither Candice nor Jillian's mother can pick up the girls at the center, and I volunteered. I'd like to take them to the park afterward, and I'd like you to come with us."

"The Fred Wallace Center," she echoed softly. "I haven't been there for years. I make annual donations to them, but the memories of Rachel working and playing in those rooms were too painful to visit. The center meant a lot to her."

"You could wait in the car," Jeff said.

She shook her head and grinned. "You see this hat? I'm going to wear it tomorrow. Time I faced old memories, and start a few new ones. Anyway, I've sometimes thought I ought to do something more for the center. Certainly I ought to be willing to visit the place."

When Jeff bid her goodnight he didn't know whether to feel hope or fear. Mother had gone through mood swings before, and she was vastly different tonight than she had been this afternoon. She sounded so much in control, totally confident and upbeat. Months of therapy were needed to bring her out of depression before. If she felt better now in a matter of hours, because of some hat, it would be a miracle. He'd have a better idea tomorrow, seeing how she handled her visit to the center and reacted to Jillian.

A phone call to Candice the next morning confirmed Jeff was set to pick up the girls at the center. So then his concern was his mother. He was relieved to see her at breakfast with spirits still high, outlook still sunny.

"I've called Harry and we have an appointment to see him at ten," she said. He was startled.

"About your job," she added. "I want to be in the first meeting you have with him, to make sure he understands the situation."

"You don't need to do that," he said.

"I don't want to diminish his authority. He's a good man. But when he retires I want you in a position to take over. That's not many years away."

He didn't trust himself to say anything beyond a muttered thanks.

She went on. "Your father was a strong-willed man, some would say stubborn. He valued college because he had to work so hard getting through, paying for everything himself."

"I understand that," he said, "and I'll take courses I need. But as you told me, I've got to do things my way."

She smiled. "What bothered him most was probably that trait you inherited from him."

"You mean I'm stubborn?"

She smiled. "Let's call it a strong will."

That afternoon he kept glancing at his mother as she sat beside him in the car. She was wearing the blue hat and talked animatedly about the times she had brought Rachel to the center. Before today, Rachel had been a subject of pain, his mother seldom mentioning her. Now the memories flowed in a gush of happy reflections. A miracle? Bless that hat.

At the center they observed the children through glass walls. Some were playing with blocks, some were painting, some were molding clay into animal forms. This was free time as contrasted to the scheduled periods of structured times under adult leadership. The mix of children was evident, with eighty percent wearing hearing equipment. Charlene seemed entranced with the activities, and spent a lot of time talking to the center's director.

Afterward the girls were glad to be taken to Chadway Park. Jillian was intrigued that Charlene could sign. Her hands flew as she tried to mouth words. At the park Charlene and Jeff sat on a wooden bench as a gusty wind periodically fanned against them from alternating directions. They were watching the girls climb up and down a multileveled platform of thick boards.

"You feel good about the meeting with Harry?" Charlene asked.

"I thought his attitude was great."

She nodded, staring at the girls for a long moment. "Did you notice how thin Jillian's legs are? Like Rachel's. She reminds me of Rachel." She was silent again, then suddenly turned toward Jeff. "I'm going to call our lawyer. I want to do something significant for the Wallace Center. And he can contact that Layhew man and give him the go-ahead on our property for Crestfield Heights."

"Are you sure?"

"As sure as I am that the future is ahead of us."

Jeff sat in wonderment. He was no doctor, and he

didn't know if his mother's new outlook was permanent or simply a phase of shifting perceptions that might later plunge toward depression. But it felt real—the way she talked, her energy and decisiveness, her optimism. But was that possible, a change so rapid that resulted in a reorientation to life? Traditional therapy was often a long, time-consuming process. But this was like a miracle. And his own outlook had changed. Another miracle?

When it was time to go Jeff helped his mother stand, and a sudden gust of wind lifted her hat and sent it careening down the path. Jeff took after it like a pit bull after a mugger. He grabbed it and brought it back to a smiling woman with an outstretched hand.

"My miracle hat," she said. Jeff didn't know much about miracles. He only knew he felt good, that he had hope and confidence for the future. Maybe that was the greatest kind of miracle that could happen to anyone.

TOUGH TOM

*I found my second miracles story stemming
from an assistant manger in Handy Dandy's, an
all-night convenience store where I occasionally
stopped for soda, peanuts, and aspirin. Tom
Dawson handled the four-to-midnight shift, so
he's the one who usually waited on me. He also
was kind of a local neighborhood celebrity, his
comic strip appearing regularly in the weekly*
Localitis *news tabloid, a free giveaway widely
distributed to every store outlet that could be
persuaded to exhibit it.* Localitis *depended on
advertisers as its sole revenue base, and naturally sought to embellish any local controversy,
event, or personality with an aura of breathless
excitement. Tom's comic strip was always
placed at the bottom of the inside back cover. It
was comprised of two strips, one on top of the
other. In the nine or ten frames Tom would develop his characters in an incident or story that
always ended with some kind of punchline. This
usually made his strip an island of comic relief
in the ocean of hyper prose surrounding the ads
and classifieds. One thing about the real Tom*

26

stood out: he looked tough, which may be why he called his strip "Tough Tom," which in itself is a little strange, because how many artists name a comic strip after themselves? Tough Tom said and did funny things, but there was usually something edgy—even abrasive—about his humor. If a certain strip took a potshot at something you liked or admired, you could end up feeling defensive. But for many readers that was part of Tough Tom's charm. He took nothing off of anybody, a character trait most readers could only fantasize they possessed. I was always curious how Tom Dawson had started the strip and what his ultimate ambition was. But I never really talked to him until something happened that led me to interview him, and I discovered a story that should begin with what happened one night while he was on a date . . .

"Are you the guy who draws this comic strip?" The man leaned over the table and looked like he was about to lose his balance. He was holding a paper. "Someone at my table told me you were Tom Dawson, who draws 'Tough Tom.' Is that right?"

Tom sighed. Not many drunks came into the Spaghetti Barn, which was one of its selling points. The other selling point was that the Barn offered the best spaghetti in town. No alcohol sold here, but you could buy something at the package liquor store half a block away and bring it in. The server would furnish a glass of ice, or a glass of no ice—whatever was wanted. So anyone really tipsy probably had a head start somewhere else before coming through the door. Too tipsy and he didn't get in. This guy had been quiet up to now, but obviously had warmed a couple of bar stools before deciding to come and damp everything down with spaghetti. Tom nodded. "Yes."

The man gestured at the paper he was holding. "You draw yourself, right? You're Tough Tom."

Tom only smiled, hoping the guy would go away.

"How tough are you?"

Tom glanced at the woman across the table. She looked worried, which increased his annoyance at the interruption. He looked back at the man. "Tough as I have to be."

A server hurriedly approached their table, taking the man's arm. "Please come back to—"

The man jerked his arm free and threw the paper down in front of Tom. "You insulted grits!" A dead silence followed, and as the server again tried to intervene, the man kept his eyes on Tom. "My mother raised me on grits. All southerners like grits."

"I don't," Tom said calmly.

"You insult all southerners."

"How's that?"

"Right here. When Tough Tom is looking at all those cars and decides on one and the dealer says if Tough Tom buys it he'll get a free bowl of grits." He pointed to the paper. "See that?"

Tom nodded.

"You remember what Tough Tom says?"

"I remember."

The man leaned forward. "Tough Tom says the best use of grits is cementing a brick outhouse. That isn't funny!"

"If you say so," Tom said.

"Your strip stinks, and you know something?" the

man went on, pushing his face close to Tom. "You stink! You're not so tough."

Tom reached out and captured the man's left index finger in a certain grip he had named the "Kenneal," taught to him by Sergeant Kenneal Black in boot camp. The man's face went pale and his left knee buckled. Slowly Tom led him back to his table, the man's mouth sucking air and unable to utter a sound. Tom gently guided the man down into his seat, then let go the finger. He smiled.

"I'm glad you like my comic strip."

As Tom returned to his table the man furiously massaged his finger.

"Sorry about that," Tom said to the woman, who still looked worried.

"You hurt him," she said.

"A little."

"You really are tough, aren't you?"

He smiled. "I let people form their own opinion."

She looked at her plate of spaghetti. "I'm—not very hungry."

"Look, Sally," he said, "let's not let my newest fan ruin our evening. He was asking for it."

She played with her fork. "You can't help it, can you? I mean—acting tough."

"How often have you seen me act tough? One time?—the fight in the parking lot after the hockey game. That guy almost ran over you." He snapped his fingers. "Oh, and the time I met you, the guy at the accident—I guess you could say I acted a little tough. You didn't seem to mind."

She kept silent, still playing with her fork. Then she looked at him. "It's not just that," shaking her head. "I don't know—I guess I've been thinking about graduation and moving to Atlanta."

"Don't remind me," he said, grinning quizzically. "Are you sure you can't get your Ph.D. at Dale-Benning?"

"You know I want my doctorate from a different school than my undergraduate degree."

He nodded. "So you've told me."

She gave a quick smile and then frowned. "You know—back on that toughness thing—I think there's something about your attitude that men sense. A kind of challenge, bringing out their macho instinct."

He was always a little uneasy when she critiqued his personality in any way. "Can't we forget that subject?"

She had spoken before about how different they were—in background and interests—and how strange their mutual attraction must seem to others. But he knew she was thinking mainly of her parents. Her talk about their differences always worried him more than when he was in Iraq during the Gulf War, driving his truck over the heat-radiating sand and trying to stay out of range of distant Iraqi tanks. But surely she realized what happened tonight wasn't his fault. Why did she springboard from that incident into a critique of his personality?

She saw the concern in his eyes and sighed, "I'm sorry."

He really couldn't blame her for thinking about their differences. He could sense how much her parents resented his seeing her. Their attitude toward him had always been coolly polite, but he could imagine their comments to her: He's not one of our kind. He's uneducated and working at Handy Dandy's, for goodness sake. What can you possibly see in him? He's not even handsome, just—big, and a little mean-looking. You have nothing in common with him.

But he did have something in common with her parents—they all thought the world of this beautiful brown-eyed woman with shoulder-length coal-black hair.

Looking at her he realized that the grits lover was not the big issue of the meal. She may have used him as a convenient excuse to say a few things she wanted him to hear. And, if so, Tom figured she had more to say. In any case, he was no longer hungry.

"Are you ready to leave?" he asked. She nodded. After paying the cashier, they passed the table of the grits man and felt him glaring after them.

They had planned on a movie after dinner, but by common consent they drove to Jackson Park, making their way up a road surrounding the circumference of a large hill, the road constricting into ever-tighter circles until the car reached the top. The large parking area was guarded by four Civil War cannons, each facing a different direction. Tom parked so they could see the downtown business district where myriad lights defined the outlines of tall buildings. Two other cars were parked across the lot, facing the manmade lake that played with light reflecting from a large monument honoring the Kentucky veterans who fought for the Union.

For a long time they sat silent. In the far distance a plane moved toward the west, white light changing to color as it faded in the distance. She spoke with a soft voice. "I'm going to start going out with Keith Sanders."

So that was it, he thought, the hidden agenda. His toughness was about to be tested, not by any sign of physical threat, but by a soft voice making a simple statement.

He breathed deeply, visualizing scenes shaped like a retrospective movie: Keith Sanders coming into Handy Dandy's shortly before midnight, grabbing a Coke and Mars bar and proclaiming he had been cramming for a calculus test he would ace; Keith Sanders, piling into the store with a carload of guys and flashing big money while buying four six-packs of beer; Keith Sanders, finding a frat brother looking at covers on the magazine rack and dragging him outside where two girls were waiting in a convertible.

He didn't like Keith Sanders, any more than Danton must have liked Robespierre while he was waiting for the guillotine.

Sally's hand crept into his, and they sat without speaking. He thought back on how he had met her, only seven months ago. She had come rushing into the store, flushed and breathing rapidly, asking to use the phone. She needed to report an accident. The details came fast: two cars a block away where a Dale-Benning University parking lot fed into Magnolia Boulevard. Her friend had hit her head. Probably not bad. Mainly shaken up. After more details she hung up the phone and thanked him, then hurried out. Tom yelled at Carrie to take over and followed the girl, quickly catching up with her.

"Are you all right?" he asked.

"Yes. I hope Janice is. Maybe now she'll listen when I tell her to fasten her seat belt. It's that jerk hitting us who bothers me most."

As they approached the scene Jeff could see a girl standing by the driver's side of a blue Ford talking to a young executive-type guy with thinning blond hair who was talking loudly and gesturing toward his car—a red Beemer.

"You didn't look," he said. "I had the right of way and you should have waited until I passed."

"I did look and didn't see you. You were going too fast. The speed limit is only thirty along here, and you were going at least forty-five."

"Oh, no," he shouted, "you're not going to sell that to the cops."

"My friend will tell them the same thing."

The man grunted in disgust. "A forty-thousand-dollar automobile messed up by a Ford." He shook his head and then looked at Sally. "Your friend pulled out right in front of me."

"The street was clear," Sally said.

"So you're going to lie, too?"

"If you had been driving at a decent speed we would have seen you coming around the curve. You had to be going over forty."

The man's face was almost as red as his car. "You're both lying bitches!"

Tom's fist moved without conscious thought, ramming directly below the point where the man's front ribs came together. The man doubled over with the giant sound of escaping air as he staggered backward two steps, hands pressed into his belly and mouth open, trying desperately to suck in new air. Then he crumpled slowly to his knees, still gasping. Tom quickly leaned forward and dragged him up, then moved him to the Ford and let him lean against it and sink into a sitting position. The man's breathing gradually built back toward normal.

"A little courtesy and respect are always helpful," Tom said.

At that moment a siren sounded the arrival of a police car. The officer got out and looked questioningly at the sitting man. Tom reached down and helped the man stand. "Just shaken up, but he'll be all right." He dusted off the man's coat. "Right, sir?"

The man mumbled, and the officer began to take their statements. Unfortunately for the man, another witness who had been waiting at the nearby bus stop confirmed that the man had been driving too fast. The officer bent down and examined the skid marks.

"We'll measure these marks and be able to tell how fast he was moving." When the officer finished asking questions and writing, Janice discovered she could drive her car, but the BMW needed a wrecker. The girls thanked Tom for his help.

"We also thank you for your ability to teach courtesy and respect," Sally grinned. "Hop in," Janice said, "we'll drive you back. By the way, what's your name?" They introduced themselves.

When Tom got out of the car his last words were, "I hope to see you again." He really didn't expect he would, but two days later one of the girls did come by—to buy a *Times-Banner,* she said. But when she paid for the paper he told her thirty-five cents wasn't enough. She looked puzzled.

"That newspaper costs two coins and a phone number," he said. The smile that lit her face made him grab a copy of *Localitis* and hold it out to her. "Use this," he said. When she finished writing she handed him the paper and then he handed her another copy of Localitis.

"Take another—it's free," he said. "And you'll especially enjoy the famous comic strip, 'Tough Tom'—inside back cover. Guaranteed to make you laugh, cry, or throw the whole thing into the trash basket."

She opened the paper. "You draw this?"

He smiled. "The editor is a friend of mine. He runs it because he doesn't have to pay me."

" 'Tough Tom,' by Tom Dawson. Are you Tough Tom? I mean—he looks like you. A little—in the face."

"I've got his muscles, too."

She laughed.

The memory faded and now as he held her hand he still had trouble believing how their relationship had developed. An unlikely duo for sure, considering their different backgrounds.

Sally Keys was twenty-two years old, a senior at Dale-Benning, an exclusive liberal arts university noted for its classical studies. She was an English Lit major who planned on teaching at the university level after getting her Ph.D. Her father was a noted dentist, a Mason, and a member of the Richview Hills Country Club; her mother was active in Eastern Star and Kiwanis and also an active supporter of the John H. Madson Center for the Homeless. Tom saw them as a typical upper-class family well accepted in society with educational and cultural interests to match.

His own background was strictly blue-collar working class. An only child, with memories of his father that made him grateful no sisters or brothers had shared his childhood years.

Ernest Dawson worked seventeen years for the Bouchard Welding and Fabricating Company before he was knifed one night in a bar fight and bled to death. He was a hard worker but when he drank he became a small child's dread of hearing heavy footfalls on the wooden porch as preamble to a blundering stagger through the house accompanied by a loud voice demanding attention from a fearful wife. Amid the swirl of loud arguments Tom would often hear the slapping sound of a hand striking a face and the muffled sobs of his mother's voice pleading for her husband to stop. Sometimes bruises would appear on her arms.

But after each hell night, the next morning demonstrated no sign of anger, no shouting or recriminations. Only the cool and remote demeanor of a man eating his breakfast and reading the sports section. Then after breakfast a kiss on his wife's cheek and a nod at his son before leaving for work.

His mother had her own way of coping. She knew how to hoard enough money to keep her special hiding place in the basement stocked with cheap wine. And Tom coped by repeating over and over to himself his mantra of survival, "Someday." Someday he would be big enough to keep his father from ever hitting his mother again. Someday he would be old enough to leave this house and never look back. Someday he would be through with school forever.

Tom hated school. His father was always complaining that he should do better, make better grades, play football and basketball, be more involved in activities, quit getting into so many fights. Nothing Tom did was good enough, and Tom learned to use school as a weapon against his father, refusing to excel at anything.

By his senior year he knew he would achieve all his short-term goals. His first goal already had been achieved—during his sophomore year. That's when his father learned to quit hitting his mother. One night when his father had hold of his mother's arms and was shouting at her, Tom had suddenly pushed between them and shoved his father backward. His father erupted and threw a wild punch at Tom, which landed on his shoulder. Tom threw a punch that missed, and the two stood toe-to-toe, hammering at each other—both too angry to be effective—until Tom landed a hard right that sent his father crashing to the floor. He lay stunned as Tom bent over him and began slapping his face with either hand, again and again, until his father's lips were splattered with blood. That's when his mother tried to make him stop, and Tom slowly pulled his father to his feet. The eyes Tom looked into no longer belonged to a drunk man.

"You will never touch my mother or me again. You will never yell or curse at either of us again. Do you understand?"

The father touched his lips with a handkerchief. He saw a son who was bigger and stronger than most sixteen-year-olds, and knew he would never again be able to whip him.

Ungrateful jerk . . . The kid had never done anything right. Wouldn't even try out for football, or any sport. Barely passing his courses. A nothing . . .

"So you think you're a tough guy?"

"Tough enough," Tom nodded. He was wary about what his father might try, but all his father did was stare at him a long moment. Then he laughed.

"You'll never amount to anything," he said, leaving the room and slamming the bedroom door behind him.

Then as Tom entered his senior year he could see the other goals close at hand—he'd soon be through with school and he could leave home. He never understood why his mother had stayed with his father all these years. Maybe she felt trapped. Or maybe her own drinking let her believe she deserved everything she got. When he suggested they both leave home after he graduated and found a job, she refused. Ernest was still her husband, and he wasn't hurting her now. He needed her, she said. So Tom planned on moving out by himself.

His mother wanted him to work and save enough money to go to college, but he had no interest in school. He had only enjoyed one course in high school, an elective art course his senior year taught by Miss Gloria Henderson. He needed an elective and thought the course would be easy. But when he got into it he found he liked it. A major emphasis in the course was commercial art, but Miss Henderson also gave assignments that tested the students' creativity and native skill for imaginative drawing. Tom liked pen and ink, and developed a stipple technique that gave depth to objects and faces. One time he drew the large head of a tiger that won an A+, and another time a school rock group asked him to design a logo that featured their name, "Five Minutes." They liked the logo and put it on tee shirts to sell. One student told Tom the shirts looked better than the band sounded.

Tom made a point of taking on extra assignments from Miss Henderson and used them as an excuse to visit with her after school. She told him that he had a natural aptitude for drawing, and hoped he would consider art as a career. But that meant more school, and he couldn't afford it anyway. He didn't have money even for a state college, much less tuition for an art school. No, he was looking forward to being free from all thoughts of school. But he told her he appreciated everything she had done for him, and was grateful for her friendship. The fact was, he realized, that he had come to think of her as a second mother as well as a teacher.

He started making drawings on his own, mostly on a sketch pad, and brought them to her for her reaction. She always encouraged him. Then one time he tried something new, bringing her on a poster board the layout of a comic strip. He had been influenced by *X-Men,* and his hero character exhibited impossible muscles as he fought alien lizard creatures to rescue a beautiful maiden. He used pen and ink with his stipple technique. Miss Henderson grinned and told him she wasn't a comic-strip expert, but the girl looked like she might need more clothing.

Now in the car Tom lightly squeezed Sally's hand as he remembered the last day of school. He had gone into Miss Henderson's room as she was getting ready to leave. She smiled a welcome and then he held before her one red rose. It was all he could afford. She exclaimed her delight, taking the rose and leaning forward to smell it. At that moment he bent over, kissing her on the cheek, and in a sudden flush her face became as red as the rose she was holding.

After graduating he enlisted in the army, figuring that was the easiest and fastest way to separate himself from his old life. During his three years in the service he wrote Miss Henderson regularly. And he maintained his interest in art, keeping a sketch pad where he captured aspects of army life and exaggerated them, building them toward caricature, more in the style of a comic strip. The mess hall, barracks, rifle range, calisthenics, KP duty, obstacle course, marching—all became grist for his developing skill. And he was developing in another way—physically. His body was filling out, and he established himself as the champion arm wrestler in his company.

He thought some about his future, and art school.

The Montgomery GI Bill would make it possible for him to go about anywhere he wanted. But the idea of school—any school—still gave him the shudders. He went to school in the army, of course, but that felt different than on the outside. Here everything was family and short term. The three years went by fast.

It was during his second year that his father got killed in a bar fight. And within another ten months his mother died of liver disease—chronic hepatitis developing into cirrhosis. Alcohol finally played its winning hand.

Tom got to attend both funerals.

By the time he mustered out he had made staff sergeant, but he was no closer to knowing what he wanted to do than when he went in. He knew he wasn't ready for school, even art school. He just wanted to get a job, make some money, meet girls, buy a new car, and have fun. So he started looking for work, but he didn't cut himself off completely from the army. He enlisted for an eight-year hitch with the reserves. One weekend a month, two weeks in the summer, and he'd have extra income while still feeling part of the family.

Job hunting was discouraging. He knew he didn't want a factory job, or a job that forced him to get dirty and wear dirty clothes. He didn't want to look like or be like his father in any way. But the nearest thing he could find to a white-collar job was an offer to enter the manager trainee program of the Handy Dandy chain. He hesitated, kept looking, but decided this was the best he could do right now.

He had been a foot soldier and proud of it. But the reserves unit in his community was a medical battalion. That's where he met Bill Vaughn, a fellow sergeant who, he found out, was starting a local news tabloid called *Localitis*.

Bill was on the lookout for writers and photographers who would work cheap. Things were going to be tight for a couple of years, but if they could hang on, he and his partner had the chance to make something worthwhile. The city had no self-promotional magazine, no real source of local journalistic pride other than the daily newspapers. And Bill's ambition not only was to start a tabloid, but to reinvest revenue into constant quality improvements until who knows where they might end? When Bill heard of Tom's interest in art, he asked to see some sketches. Tom furnished some, along with a sample comic strip he called "Tough Tom."

Bill was doubtful at first, but he asked for more sample strips. He liked the edge to Tom's humor, the offbeat reactions of the characters, the sudden pouncing double entendres that could jar readers with a surprised awareness. Not always mainline humor, but *Localitis* was not exactly *Reader's Digest* circulation, either. Why not try it?

The deal was made with a handshake. *Localitis* would carry a comic strip with the title "Tough Tom."

Tom enjoyed the transition from foot soldier to being a truck driver in the reserves. His three years in the regular army had demanded no response to foreign conflicts. Then, ironically, during his first year back in civilian life he got shipped to the Gulf War. That's when he saw enough sun and sand to point all future vacations toward snow-capped mountains. The only wounded he personally touched was a squad of mangled bodies hit by friendly fire from a U.S. tank.

When he got home he was anxious to see Miss

Henderson. She now had retired from teaching, so that she focused more time on their relationship that had grown ever more warm and affectionate. She wanted to hear all about his experiences in the Gulf, and his free mornings gave him the chance to visit her often. She returned the favor by frequently coming to the store, although it was far from her neighborhood.

The one uneasy subject between them was her displeasure of his job. She felt he should be going to school. And now with the government willing to finance his education, she couldn't understand why he was satisfied to drift. He wouldn't stay happy where he was. He was wasting time and going nowhere, and the longer he put off school the harder it would be to get started.

He could say little to her when she talked like that. Logic weighed in on her side of the argument. But logic doesn't move the heart, and he only knew he couldn't stand the thought of school, or any other kind of change. Not now. Was he drifting, or simply taking time to smell the roses? He only knew that he was content. And even if he *were* drifting, he wanted nothing to rock the boat.

But now Sally was rocking the boat, creating a tidal wave with two little words, "Keith Sanders."

Tom's mind began playing with the idea. Okay. So she wanted to date the all-American college guy. Not a new idea exactly. She had dated him in high school. The thing was—Sally and Keith had a lot in common. As Sally explained it one time when they were dawdling over coffee after a steak dinner, her family and Keith's had known each other for years before Keith's father—an insurance executive—got transferred to the company's home headquarters located in

Dallas. The families were in church together, seeing each other every week, and Sally had dated Keith during their freshman year in high school before the move. Years later when Keith returned to attend Blake University—a much larger school than Dale-Benning—he tried to get with Sally again. But the chemistry seemed different, and they drifted apart long before Tom loaned Sally his phone. So now maybe Sally and Keith were drifting together again?

Tom wasn't buying it.

"Why?"

"Why what?" she asked.

"Why the games?"

She glanced quickly at him. "What do you mean?"

"Don't we know each other well enough to say what's really on our minds?"

She sat silent, then slowly nodded. "I want us to quit going steady. To see other people."

After a moment he said, "So you really want to start dating Keith Sanders?"

"We can still keep seeing each other occasionally," she said.

"And then you can see some other guys besides Keith and me?—kind of loosen things up because you're going to be focusing on graduate school and you don't need the distraction of some guy who happens maybe to be falling in love with you?"

"Tom, please—" she said.

"Look," he said, "I know we're an odd couple, as far as anyone else looking at us. Your parents don't like me. I understand that. I guess to them I'm some slum guy reaching above his station. And they're right about one thing, because I do hold you higher than myself. You're smarter than I am, better than I am in every way I can think of. I don't know why you like me, but I'm glad you do. I don't worry about the rest. And tomorrow—I don't know about tomorrow, but I do know about today, and life is one day at a time. I learned that years ago. You seize the moment and squeeze every last ounce of happiness out of it, and then the next day you do the same. And somehow the future takes care of itself. No matter what you do or where you go tomorrow, it doesn't have to change anything today. I don't want to share you with Keith Sanders or anyone else."

She looked away from him, staring through the windshield at the downtown city lights. His gaze followed her view, and he focused on a pulsating beacon that seemed to echo the rapid beating of his heart. Finally she turned to him again, her eyes glazed with moistness.

"I thought it would be easier this way than waiting until the last moment to say good-bye. I don't like good-byes. Good-byes hurt. I wanted to soften it, ease into it, make it easier to leave when the time comes." She smiled. "But I was wrong, wasn't I?"

Something alerted within him, as though he were suddenly listening to a new song. He slowly grinned at her. "Wait a minute," he said, "is Keith Sanders already history?"

"Keith Sanders was never going to happen."

"Un-huh," he said, "and what is going to happen?"

She laughed. "What happens is what we make happen."

He sat there, almost afraid to move. She brought his hand to her face then. "Silly man, I haven't thought of another man since I met you."

"Really?" he asked.

Her nose crinkled. "Really."

With a whoop and a hug he grabbed her to him

and began the most fierce mouth-to-mouth resuscitation campaign in the history of human endeavor. Finally, breathless, she pulled away.

"But this doesn't change the fact that I'm going to school, getting my Ph.D., and teaching in a university. And the day is coming when we'll have to say good-bye. You understand that?"

He nodded.

"Okay," she said, "But this is the present, and like you say we can be honest with each other and squeeze as much happiness as we can out of each day. So—do you know one major reason why I like you?"

"Because I'm tough?"

She laughed. "Because you're a tender man who makes me feel totally secure. We're going to play this your way, Buster, so enjoy it." She put her arms around his neck and gently pulled him to her.

He did enjoy it.

The next afternoon when Tom reported for work he saw Howie Martin bent under the counter working with a hammer.

"What're you doing?"

Howie looked up and glanced around. No one else was in the store. "I'm building a small shelf for our gun."

"It's safer kept in the office," Tom said.

"But this is where we can get at it, if anyone tries to make us open the safe."

Tom shook his head. "Bad idea."

"You never know when you'll need it. The Macon Road store got hit last night."

"Anybody hurt?"

"No, but when two guys didn't get much from the

safe, they tore up the place. I don't want that to happen here."

"Okay," Tom said. "But I'd still feel better if the gun were in the office."

As time passed, Tom tried not to think of Sally's departure. Of course, saying good-bye did not mean he would no longer see her. A long drive to Atlanta, but one he could make on weekends. Adding to his contentment was the way Sally and Miss Henderson got along. Miss Henderson certainly approved of Sally, and had invited them both to her home for dinner a number of times. And she went with Tom to see Sally graduate.

They sat at the back of the audience, and afterward as the crowd stood in scattered groups they made their way forward to where Sally was talking to her parents. She greeted Tom with a big smile and a quick hug. Over her shoulder Tom saw her father grimace. But then the parents were unceasingly polite in exchanging pleasantries.

One night two weeks before Sally was to leave for Atlanta he was particularly tired working the second shift. He was fighting off some kind of bug, and Carrie complained of the same thing. She was obviously in worse shape than he, and he let her go home early, his watch showing 10:39. Less than an hour and a half until he could also leave.

He watched Carrie climb into her ten-year-old Dodge and then leave, passing a classic Mustang with gold hubcaps. The Mustang drove slowly into the parking lot, moving directly toward the entrance and at the last moment turning and leaving Tom's line of sight. Then another car cut into the parking lot, one Tom recognized immediately. Miss Henderson in her old brown Toyota Celica ST she had bought new many years ago. It had been in countless body shops, painted three times, and still carried Miss Henderson wherever she wanted.

"A little late for you to be coming by, isn't it?" he asked when she came bustling through the door.

"Yes—but I need to make a dessert for my bridge club that meets tomorrow, and I changed my mind on what to make. I need to melt some caramels."

Tom grinned. Handy Dandy had, if nothing else, every kind of candy known in the civilized world. He was moving over to the candy display when the front door burst open and a man stood on widespread legs with arms straight out and both hands holding a gun pointed directly at him.

"Don't move!" The man was wearing a ski mask.

Tom froze, but his brain was already hitting fourth gear, already thinking of the gun Howie had put under the counter.

The man looked at Miss Henderson. "Give me the purse. Hurry!" She held it to him and he jerked it open, grabbing her wallet and spilling everything else to the floor. Then he looked back at Tom.

"You'd better hope you've got more money in that safe than she has in this purse, or you're dead. Now move!"

Tom started walking slowly, hoping the man would grow impatient and come closer. But the man stayed out of range and then moved quickly to Miss Henderson, holding her head and jamming his gun against her throat. "I said move fast or she starts talking with metal in her voice box."

Tom moved rapidly toward the safe.

"Wait a minute!" the man shouted. "Not you. She opens the safe. You tell her the combination."

Tom stopped walking and turned toward the man.

"You let her go or you won't see the inside of that safe."

The man pushed Miss Henderson away and again gripped the gun in both hands, pointing it at Tom. "I'll shoot you, man! I'll shoot you in the shoulders, in the arms, in the legs until you tell her the combination. I'm the king, man, and you're going to do it my way. Right now!"

He took careful aim, and at that moment a can of dog food flew past his face, narrowly missing him. He whirled quickly and shot. Miss Henderson jerked backward into the candy rack and Tom launched himself at the man's legs. The man turned and fired again, and Tom felt the bullet sing past his ear as he plowed against the man's legs. They both went down, crashing into a pyramid display of Bud beer.

They threshed among the cans and Tom grabbed the wrist of the gun hand, squeezing and twisting and butting his head into the man's chin. The gun flew to the floor. Then Tom creased his fingers at the first knuckle, making a solid wedge which he rammed hard into the man's throat.

The man quit struggling, gasping for air, but Tom was already leaning over Miss Henderson. Her shoulder was bleeding, but she was smiling. "I'm sorry I missed him. I never was a good softball player."

Tom tore off his shirt and placed it over her wound. "Can you hold this?" he asked. She nodded and he went to the phone and dialed 911. After relaying information, he went back to the man, who was still struggling to breathe. Tom touched his throat, then moved back to Miss Henderson.

"Is he all right?" she asked.

He nodded. "I'll think he'll survive, but that blow

can be fatal. It can crush the larynx and create a swelling where he can't get air to his lungs."

Her eyes closed, and he spoke gently. "You saved my life, Miss Henderson."

She looked at him then, and spoke without smiling. "Tom Dawson, I will not have saved your life until you go to school and become the artist God meant for you to be."

Looking down at her it seemed like he had never heard anything before. And it was suddenly clear. He could see everywhere he had been, everything he had done. The fearful child huddled under his blankets and dreading the sound of heavy footsteps on the front porch, the growing boy feeling inadequate and unworthy under the constant assault of criticism, the teenager turning his back on all the opportunities of school in ultimate rebellion—they were gone. No more doubts, no more indecision. He was going to go to the art school in Atlanta, not because of Miss Henderson and his regard for her, not because of his feeling for Sally and the desire to be near her in Atlanta, but because—and this was the real miracle—he wanted it!

LARRY'S JUMP

I first met Larry Whittaker when I visited Whittaker Farms. I had learned the Methodist churches were going to hold a combined Easter sunrise service out there with the bishop coming as principal speaker. I wanted to run a feature article and scout out the place for taking some photos. While there I met the Whittakers and their children. One child especially interested me, seventeen-year-old Larry. I was introduced to him in a room loaded with the ultimate in computer equipment. I learned he was a real computer buff—almost a prodigy. He had already written some programs that his father used in tracking the stock market and in cataloging and operating his cacti greenhouse collection. Larry's language of choice was C++, but he also knew Visual BASIC and had worked with Assembler. I mentioned I was thinking of getting a new computer for home use, and he started talking about a Pentium computer with a PCI bus. I took him quickly to the idea that I was only interested in word processing and didn't want to spend a lot of money. The fact is

*at home I was still using an old Compaq with
an 8086 chip, and I was tired of waiting twenty-
four seconds for the program to load. I could
tell Larry hated lowering his thought process to
so mundane a challenge, but he acknowledged I
could get by with a 386SX chip going 33MHz.
And please, no less than 4Mb RAM. He said the
new computer could probably load my word
processor in less than three seconds. I followed
his advice, but I might never have come in contact with Larry again had I not heard nine
months later what happened to Mr. Whittaker's
collection of cacti. Then I discovered the story
of my third miracle . . .*

The air was gushing through the open exit of the
Cessna 182 as Larry stood poised beside his brother.
He looked forward to the jump, but he wasn't happy
with Wayne's challenge. Why did he let Wayne talk
him into this? They were nearly at ten thousand feet,
which would give them about fifty seconds of free-
fall. Wayne nodded impatiently toward the open air.
Larry glanced at the altimeter on his wrist that would
let him know when to pull the rip cord, no later than
three to two thousand feet for a safe opening. But today Wayne had dared Larry not to open his chute until Wayne did. Larry knew this meant Wayne would
be pressing toward the two-thousand-foot level.
Wayne nodded again at the exit. Larry launched himself out and immediately forgot his worry in the ex-
hilaration of total freedom. He arched his back with
arms and legs spread as Wayne moved beside him
and then separated further away. Wayne did a backward somersault, and Larry did the same. Then they

both did a forward somersault, ending up facing down. Now Wayne moved still farther away, and suddenly ducked his head, lowered his arms to his sides, and accelerated in a rapid descent. Larry quickly followed him, feeling the wind stiffen against his face. Wayne then lifted his arms and arched his body, slowing his descent. Larry caught up to him, slowing his own descent. He reached out and shook Wayne's hand.

Larry felt close to his brother. One year younger, he had followed Wayne through the process of growing up. They had played together, exploring every rock, tree, and stream that comprised the two hundred acres of Whittaker Farms, its woods and rolling hills accessorized with long wooden fences and a variety of obstacle jumps for the horses stabled there.

When the boys were big enough to ride, Wayne was always the one who rode faster and took the biggest jumps. He was the one who came up with the ideas of what to do next. Larry naturally accepted his brother's greater size and strength and daring. Only with computers did he feel superior to Wayne.

Right now Larry was watching his altimeter as the two of them plummeted toward the earth. He pointed to his wrist but Wayne ignored him. Larry had lost all sensation of falling, feeling as though he were in the air while the earth rose to meet him.

Then he saw his altimeter hit three thousand feet, and he waved at Wayne and pointed to his wrist. Wayne only grinned as he, too, watched his altimeter. Twenty-five hundred feet. Pull the cord, Larry thought. Wayne kept falling. They were closing in on two thousand feet. *Now, pull now!* Two thousand feet. Larry wildly gestured to Wayne. The earth was now huge and rushing ever more rapidly toward them. In desperation Larry yanked his rip cord and felt the sudden strong jerk upward on his harness, followed by the great relief of the slow, gentle, controlled floating that was the hallmark of his Falcon chute. Then, looking down, he saw Wayne's chute blossom below him.

They landed lightly on their feet within twenty yards of each other.

"What did you think?" Wayne asked, smiling.

"You know what I think," Larry said. "Are you trying to kill yourself?"

"Hey—do I sense a little panic in your voice?"

They were rolling up their chutes. "Not for myself," Larry said. "I'd prefer my brother to eat pancakes, not be one."

Wayne shrugged. "I had a lock on it all the way."

"You pushed it too far."

Wayne shook his head. "Don't sweat it. As long as you follow what I do, you'll be all right."

They started walking to the hangar as their Cessna was making a landing.

"Are you mad because you pulled before me?" Wayne asked.

"I'm mad because you pulled late."

Wayne laughed. "Look, little brother. I know you can't do everything the way I do. But you try, so don't be down on yourself for panicking a little."

"I didn't panic."

"Yeah, the way you didn't panic when I introduced you to Eilene last week."

Larry groaned to himself. He had been eating with his brother in the school cafeteria when Eilene Jacobs came through the line with Barbara Medlin.

"There she is," Larry said, nudging Wayne.

"Not bad," Wayne said. "A little thin for my taste."

"She's in my French class, but I haven't had the guts to introduce myself."

"Easier than jumping out of an airplane." Wayne drained the last of his Coke. "Back in a moment," he said, standing.

"Where are you going?" Larry grabbed his arm.

"I know Barbara. I'll invite them over."

"No!"

Wayne grinned. "Do I sense fear and panic?"

"Sit down, please."

"Relax," Wayne said, "you're my brother, and I've always taken care of you. So it's time once again." He started to walk away, then paused, "Besides, dear brother, remember the words my history teacher once quoted from Bovee, 'Good men have the fewest fears.' "

Larry felt his heart beating faster as he watched Wayne talking to Barbara, and even faster when both girls turned and looked toward his table. Then the three of them moved toward him. He didn't know whether to stand or keep sitting. If only he could be like Wayne—no one was cooler around girls.

"Eilene and Barbara, this is my brother, Larry. He's a computer genius."

Larry felt himself blushing as he stood and stammered a greeting. He pushed his chair to one side and moved his tray. Then, straightening up, his hand brushed his glass of milk, and with horror he watched it splash over his salad. When the commotion settled and they were talking, Larry was delighted to learn Eilene was also interested in computers—principally desktop publishing. She was thinking of a career in journalism.

He also learned she was interested in acting, and was planning to try out for the spring play. And at the end of lunch, he knew once again that his brother had done what he himself could not have done. Thanks to him, Larry knew someone he wanted to know even better.

Now, riding home in the Ford pickup, Larry rolled up his window against the air, which was rapidly turning colder. "I don't think we should tell mother about the jump today."

"She knew we were jumping."

"You know what I mean."

Wayne laughed. "You don't want me to tell her how you panicked and opened early?"

"I mean I don't want her to be more worried than she already is."

Wayne swerved around a pothole. "She's accepted our skydiving."

"Yeah, after making sure we had the best instruction and bought the best equipment and then got independent reports from two different instructors. You don't think she's worried?"

"Okay. Maybe she's a little worried, but at least Dad's okay with it."

They rode in silence a few moments, then Larry spoke in a quiet voice. "I think he's also concerned."

"Why do you say that?"

"The last time I was in the greenhouse he asked if I ever got afraid when skydiving."

Wayne shook his head. "He sure hasn't said anything to me, but then," he glanced at Larry, "you're the one he talks to."

"What do you mean?"

"You've always been his favorite."

"That isn't true."

"Think about it—who does he take into the green-house and share tales about his beloved cacti?"

"He's taken you into the greenhouse."

"Very little."

"Maybe that's because he thought you were never interested."

Wayne scoffed. "Who would be. Cacti? I saw all the cacti I wanted when I fell on one that summer at the horse ranch in Colorado."

"Cacti are more than sharp needles. You've seen the wide variety of flowers he grows."

Wayne snorted. "They're still ugly."

"But you've got to admire what he's done," Larry said. "His cacti collection is the most extensive in the Southeast."

Wayne laughed drily. "His horse farm is also one of the best, but he's more interested in growing that new cactus hybrid than in knowing what mare is go-ing to foal." He shook his head. "Without Ed and George running the operation, this place would be nowhere."

"He keeps up with what's going on."

Wayne reached over and rested his hand on Larry's shoulder. "I guess we can't agree on everything." He smiled. "Just almost everything."

At home the smell of roast beef met them when they stepped into the kitchen. Agnes was bending over the oven, and their mother was carefully check-ing the vegetables.

"Larry," she said, "your father wants you to come to the greenhouse."

Wayne raised his eyebrows at Larry, then kissed his mother on the forehead. "I'm going to the stables to see Mandarin."

"Dinner will be ready in twenty minutes," his mother said.

As the boys left the house Wayne grinned, "Give the cacti my love."

If the choice was between being affectionate to cacti or a horse, Larry knew Wayne would have the easier time. Mandarin was a two-year-old filly foaled here and practically hand-raised by Wayne. She had a black coat, solid but trim build, and could run with easy abandon. She could also jump, and Wayne never looked happier than when he was taking her over the hedge obstacles that formed part of the training ground.

In the greenhouse Larry saw his father studying a thermometer. He greeted Larry with a frown. "Three degrees variance from the other thermometers."

Larry knew his dad was fussy about the temperature. If the temperature in the greenhouse ever dropped below fifty degrees an alarm system would let him know inside the house.

His father shook his head and bent over a plant which Larry recognized was the *Melocactus* that contained a *Phyllocactus* graft.

The *Phyllocactus* was his father's favorite cactus. His collection included numerous examples of this genus. Imported from Brazil, it differed greatly from the appearance of the flattened branch species so prevalent in the western states. Its flowers ranged from crimson to rose pink to creamy white. His father had described it as the most ornamental of all cacti, making the most beautiful garden plants.

The greenhouse contained examples of one or more species from almost every known genus of cactus: the *Melocactus*, growing from one to two feet high; the *Mammillaria*, mainly found in Mexico, with white and yellow tints predominating; the *Cereus,* which in native soil can grow to a height of fifty feet; the *Epiphyllum,* from Brazil; the *Rhipsalis,* from Central America; the *Opuntia,* from the West Indies; the *Pilocereus;* the *Echinopsis;* and all of them carefully nurtured in a temperature-controlled environment.

Larry had asked his father how he had got interested in cacti, and his father related how on a trip to Mexico he noticed a number of natives using strange-looking toothpicks. He found out the toothpicks were actually spines from the *E.ingens* species of the *Echinocactus* genus. This species grew large, and it was estimated fifty thousand spines existed on a single plant. His father began investigating other genera of cacti and became interested in starting his own collection.

Now his father looked at his watch. "Almost time for dinner. How about checking behind me on the alarm system?"

Larry nodded. He wasn't an expert on alarm systems, but ever since he had shown his affinity for computers, his father thought that somehow qualified him on other things electrical. Wayne was right about one thing—his father *had* spent more time with his cacti and his horse farm than with his children growing up. But Larry did appreciate his father's intellectual curiosity about cacti and his desire to become an expert in the field. After all, both he and Wayne wanted to be expert in their own fields—he, computer programming and Wayne, animal husbandry.

Dinner proved that Agnes could still make the best pot roast in the universe. Talk ranged from the weather—unseasonably cold for Kentucky—to the Kimber Blue Ball, an annual event held at the Rich

Meade Country Club in honor of Kimber Blue, a great three-year-old champion for Cross Creek Farms in the 1920s. Tradition decreed that the women wear some shade of blue in their formal gowns, and those attending comprised the most prominent families in horse breeding and racing from the central-state area. Sixteen was the magic age for sons or daughters to be invited, so Larry and Wayne both qualified. Why an occasion to honor one horse when so many other great horses had raced in the last seventy years, no one seemed to care. The Kimber Blue Ball had become the *crème de la crème* fall season event.

"Do you boys have dates for the ball?" their mother asked.

"I'm taking Sandra Graves," Wayne said.

"Larry?"

"I was thinking of not going."

His mother stared at him. "Why on earth not? When you were fifteen you were mad you couldn't go."

He grinned. "That was because I was too young. When I went last year I wasn't thrilled."

She smiled. "Maybe you were with the wrong girl."

"Mary Pearson was all right." Larry piled another piece of meat on his plate. "Everyone seemed so—stiff. Like they were speaking memorized lines."

"Larry may have a better time this year," Wayne said.

Mother raised her eyebrows. "Why is that?"

Wayne grinned. "A girl in his French class."

"What's her name?"

Wayne nodded to Larry, who muttered, "Eilene Jacobs."

"I haven't heard you speak of her."

"She moved from Denver just before school started. Her father's an executive at CompuCorp."

Mother smiled. "Computers. How interesting."

"She likes computers, too."

"Sounds like you might have a lot in common."

"She also likes to ride horses," Wayne said.

"How do you know?" Larry asked.

Wayne grinned. "Hey, I talk to her, too."

"Have you met her parents?" Mother asked.

Larry shook his head. "I just really started talking to her last week, and our only date was after school when we had a Coke at the Double Straw."

Mother patted her mouth with a napkin. "Why don't you invite her here for a ride?"

"Gonzi would be a good choice for her if she's an occasional rider," their father added. Gonzi was an eight-year-old chestnut filly with a tame disposition.

"Speaking of horses, Dad," Wayne broke in, "has Mr. Fielding said anything yet about Mandarin?"

Father nodded. "He's changed his mind. Told me today he wants to take her."

"No!"

"I'm sorry Wayne, but it's out of my hands."

"Don't sell her; she's my horse!"

His father sighed, "We've already been over this. You've known since she was foaled that Mr. Fielding was planning to buy her."

"He wanted Mandarin for his daughter, and she's gotten married and moved to Michigan."

"I asked you not to get too attached to Mandarin."

"But why does he want Mandarin now?"

His father put down his napkin and looked directly at Wayne. "Roy is a very dear friend of mine and I promised him the first filly sired by Kimmer out of Maywind. Our deal was a handshake, and it was understood if the filly looked good and trained right, he would have the chance to buy her. I've made this clear to you. He wanted us to break in the filly. She's ready now, in large measure thanks to you."

Father took a sip of coffee. "It's true, when his daughter married he almost changed his mind. But he's built a new horse barn and with his nephew coming to stay with him next summer he wants to buy Mandarin."

"Then offer to buy her back. Let him have another horse."

"There's no way I can do that."

Wayne stood. "You don't care about what I want. All you care about is the cacti. You don't even like the horses. Your grandfather and father built this farm, but for you it's just a way to make money." He turned and rushed from the room.

"Wayne!" his father yelled, standing. His wife grabbed his arm.

"Let him go, Edward. Give him a chance to cool down. You can talk later."

Larry stood, and his father looked at him. "Where are you going?"

"He really loves Mandarin," Larry said, and left the room. Slowly his father sank back into his chair, and stared at his wife.

"Horses are easier to raise than boys," he said finally. Then he stood again and walked over to a table standing near a window and picked up a pot containing a species of *Mammillaria*, with purple flowers rising from the upper part of the stem. He looked closely at the yellow-tinted spines. Then he set the cactus down and faced his wife.

"Wayne knew, all the time, that Mandarin was promised to someone else."

"Knowing doesn't always force the heart to accept."

He smiled. "A truth well spoken deserves a better answer than I can give. And frankly, I have no answer to Wayne. I know we've been growing apart. I just don't know what to do about it."

"The irony is that he loves horses as much as your father did."

He nodded and moved back to the table, sinking into the chair. "I hate to see him so upset."

She reached out and put her hand over his. "Then let me say something. I'm not as worried about Wayne as I am about Larry."

He was surprised. "Larry's doing fine."

She was silent for a long moment, looked down at the table, then back up at him. "I think Larry may be—too close to Wayne."

"They've always been close."

"When they were growing up that seemed all right. Wayne was older, the natural leader. And he involved Larry in a lot of activities. You hear stories about sibling rivalry, but there's never been a hint of that with them. I just think Larry is old enough now to start going his separate way.

"Larry has gone into computers where Wayne has no interest. And he has shown no inclination, like Wayne, for the business of raising and training horses. But in so many other ways he's still dependent on Wayne. He follows Wayne's lead in just about everything."

He looked away from her, thinking. "Perhaps you're right, but I hadn't seen that as a problem."

"You saw him after Wayne left the table. He took Wayne's side."

"I can understand that."

"Do you remember when they ever had a fight?" He shook his head.

"When they even had a loud argument?"

"No," he admitted.

"Well, dear," she said, standing and collecting some plates, "I'm no marriage counselor, but I think our sons could use a divorce—from each other."

Larry followed Wayne to the barn where Mandarin was stabled. As he got closer he saw Wayne stroking Mandarin's nose and talking softly to her. Larry paused and listened, barely able to make out the words: ". . . he doesn't understand. You're my horse, and he's going to sell you. But he has no right. He'll be sorry. He's never had to lose something he really loved. But someday he'll understand. I promise you that . . ."

Larry cleared his throat. Wayne was startled. "What do you want?"

"I just wanted to say I'm sorry. He shouldn't sell the horse."

"He'll be sorry."

"What do you mean?"

"I don't know how, but someday I'll make him sorry."

Larry moved up to Mandarin and began rubbing her neck. "The thing is—Dad always keeps his word, even when he's wrong."

"He doesn't have to sell Mandarin."

Larry kept rubbing Mandarin's neck, saying nothing.

Wayne suddenly grinned and jabbed Larry's shoulder. "So, Bro—we've got to stick together, right?" He went into a mock fighting stance and began shadowboxing at Larry. "No matter what the old man does, or anyone else, or anything else that happens. We're together, right?"

Larry slowly nodded.

The next day Larry asked Eilene to meet him at the Double Straw after school. He got there first, sitting at a booth near the front. He liked this place, named after a relic from a past era when it was always more cool to drink from a double straw than the inferior single straw. The walls were covered with posters of old Coke ads, big automobiles, and bare legs with bobby socks and penny loafers.

Larry ordered a couple of Cokes and then saw her come in, happy that her face lit in a big smile when she saw him wave.

As they talked Larry had the feeling they had known each other a long time. Very strange. Then he told her about the Kimber Blue Ball. She looked curiously at him.

"The gowns have to be blue?"

"Some blue in them," he said, "but I'll be blue if you don't go with me."

She laughed. "You're funny all right. But we hardly know each other and you're talking about a formal ball?"

"We can take care of that knowing part. How about coming to my place on Saturday for a ride on Gonzi?"

"Gonzi?"

"A great little filly."

She looked at him thoughtfully. "You know, my parents need to meet you."

"I'm willing."

"Why do I get the idea you're trying to speed up things?"

He grinned. "Have you looked in the mirror lately?"

She drank the last of her Coke. "Okay, let me ask mother if I can invite you for dinner Saturday night."

"After riding with me?"

She nodded.

"Sounds great," he said. "But who's trying to speed things up now?"

She smiled. "Have you looked in the mirror lately?"

As he watched the highlights from the overhead lamp play off her dark hair, he had the sudden thought he was falling harder and faster than in any other jump he had made, and this time he didn't have a chute.

When Larry told Wayne about Eilene's coming to ride on Saturday, Wayne looked disgruntled.

"Not this Saturday," he said. "I wanted us to take some jumps."

"No time. After riding I've been invited to her place for dinner."

Wayne raised his eyebrows. "Sounds like you're riding on a fast track."

"And I've asked her to the Kimber Blue Ball."

"Okay, so you'll be with Eilene on Saturday. How about bringing her to the field instead? She can watch our jumps."

"I promised her a ride on Gonzi."

Wayne threw up his hands. "I know when I'm licked."

"You can ride with us."

"No thanks," Wayne shook his head. "I'm going to go diving."

On Saturday Larry took Eilene to the house where he introduced her to his parents.

"And bring her into the greenhouse when you finish your ride," his father said.

Eilene was a little nervous when moving into the saddle, but not a move or quiver betrayed any uncertainty in Gonzi as Eilene settled on her back. She seemed to regard Eilene with the patience of a lenient tutor.

"How did she get that name?" Eilene asked.

"Eight years ago when she was foaled, a man with his small daughter was visiting dad. Dad took them to the stable to see the filly, and the little girl named her."

Eilene looked puzzled.

"The girl was so excited she kept saying over and over while she walked, 'Goin-see, goin-see.' "

" 'Gonzi'?"

"That's what it sounded like. Gonzi. Dad said that's what he'd name her."

Eilene's initial nervousness soon faded. She expressed her admiration for the beauty of the place, the horses, the stables and landscaping. Larry showed off a little by jumping over two hedge obstacles. She was properly impressed.

When they finished riding Larry said, "Now for the climax of your visit. Dad's famous cacti collection."

Inside the greenhouse they saw his father working over a plant. He gave Eilene a brief tour of the greenhouse, and then moved the couple back to his original plant.

"This is my big project right now," he said, "This *Melocactus.*" He pointed to a roundish plant about two feet high, with the tip of the plant ending in a circular crown of about five inches. Small pink flowers grew from the crown.

"Natives in the West Indies eat this cactus. It has a slightly acid flavor but still tastes pretty good. What I'm trying to do with this specimen is create a new variety of cactus by combining the *M. communis* species of *Melocactus* with the *Phyllocactus.*"

Later, as Eilene slid behind the steering wheel of her car, she said, "Remember, dinner at eight. My folks are anxious to meet you."

"Looking forward to it. And—" he hesitated, "—I'm sorry if Dad got carried away by cacti."

"I enjoyed learning about cacti. Anyway," she smiled, "you'll probably be hearing a lot about computers tonight."

"At least computers are where I am."

"You're lucky computers aren't prickly."

Larry smiled. "That has never bothered Dad." With a wave she accelerated away, leaving him to ponder why this had been one of the greatest days of his life.

During the next few weeks his relationship with Eilene blossomed as rewardingly as his father's cacti. Then on a Saturday one week before the Kimber Blue Ball Mr. Fielding came after Mandarin. His father had warned Wayne a week earlier. Larry could almost feel Wayne count the hours that last week, and as the day drew nearer Larry got more worried about what Wayne's reaction might be when the horse trailer arrived.

Larry looked at his watch. 8:00 A.M. Mr. Fielding was prompt as he pulled up to the stables. His father smiled in greeting as Mr. Fielding got out. Larry looked around for Wayne, whom he hadn't seen since breakfast. Two stableboys helped load Mandarin into the trailer. Larry walked back toward the house and saw Wayne standing on the front porch, leaning against a post. He was staring toward the stables.

As Larry got nearer he was struck by Wayne's expression. There was none. His face was absolutely blank, with eyes cold as an arctic blizzard. Wayne made no move as the trailer pulled away along the driveway. His head followed the trailer as it moved down the highway, becoming nothing but a speck that vanished behind an oak tree. His father approached the house and began moving up the steps. He stopped beside Wayne, about to say something, but Wayne moved past him and away from the house as though his father didn't exist.

Larry ran down the steps. "Wayne!" he yelled. "Let's do some jumps." Wayne kept moving toward the stables.

The night of the Kimber Blue Ball was captured by a severe cold front that blasted in from the Northeast. Before donning his overcoat, scarf, and gloves Larry had to admit that the image he gave to the full-length mirror wasn't bad. Five feet eleven, 180 pounds, and dark blond hair with a slight natural wave. And his parents didn't look shabby, either. His mother was a knockout in a light blue floor-length gown. And his father—not bad for a slightly overweight guy who raises cacti. The only shadow on the household was cast by Wayne's refusal to attend the ball. He had canceled out on Sandra Graves three weeks ago. He was still not speaking to his father. But Larry tried to brush aside his concern for Wayne in the anticipation of seeing Eilene.

That anticipation increased as he greeted Eilene's parents and waited with them in the living room for her to appear. His anticipation kept building as he watched the empty stairs leading up to her dressing room. Suddenly he saw a vision coming down slowly, and he appreciated that the delayed and slow entrance was for his benefit. She was wearing an indigo taffeta slim-skirted gown with one shoulder bare. Her hair was loose and flowing, and the sight of it brushing her bare shoulder excited him to the degree his tongue stumbled over his words of greeting. His eyes spoke for him, though, and what they said heightened the smile of her face.

At the entrance to the Rich Meade Country Club he felt like a prince with his princess as he handed his printed invitation to the doorman. Inside he saw people he knew; later saw his parents mingling with perfect ease. Once he saw Sandra Graves with her new date, Harold Knight, brushing by him with an angry stare. And as the evening passed amid the moving array of colorful gowns, flashing jewelry, and men's formalwear, he felt part of an ancient pageantry reserved strictly for royalty.

But the moment when he felt most exalted came under soft lights on the dance floor, surrounded by the lush sound of a full orchestra playing "Stardust." He held Eilene close, undulating in slow motion with his heart timed to the music, the side of his face rested against hers. He could feel the pulse in her temple. Then without conscious thought his head slowly sank down until his lips made contact with her bare shoulder, and the taste of her skin, combined with the scent of her perfume, made the room spin. When his head finally raised and his eyes looked deep into hers, he felt his arms pull her even closer, making it easier for his lips gently to meet hers, and suddenly he was at ten thousand feet, ready for the jump.

When Larry got home after the ball he saw lights

on in the greenhouse and found his father looking at the thermometer. "The temperature has dropped another ten degrees outside," his father said. "I'm glad we have the new alarm system."

"Don't worry, Dad," Larry said. "Our generator's ready to kick in if anything happens to the power."

His father nodded. "That cold outside would kill all my cacti if something went wrong." He cut off the lights and walked with Larry toward the house.

"Eilene is a beautiful girl," his father said, "and you two made a striking couple."

"Thanks, Dad. Would you think I'm crazy if I said I think I love her? Not knowing her any longer than I have?"

"Not crazy, but you're still very young. You may not believe it, but love may come many times before you're ready to make a commitment to one woman."

"I know I'm not ready for that kind of commitment, but I don't think I'll never feel stronger about any other woman than I feel right now for Eilene."

His father patted him on the shoulder. "You've still got a long ride ahead of you, Son. Just keep a loose rein and have faith the horse knows the way home. You'll make it to where you need to be."

Sunday morning was usually a relaxed time— everybody laid back around a late breakfast. But the moment Larry entered the breakfast room he knew something was wrong. Agnes wasn't serving. His father and mother were missing. Only Wayne was there, sitting at the table and eating a grapefruit. He gave Larry a big smile.

"Good morning, Bro. Want some grapefruit? I left a half for you."

"Where is everybody?"

"I think they're in the greenhouse." He took a sip

of coffee. "Man, I can't make coffee as good as Agnes."

"What's wrong?"

Wayne sighed. "I don't have the touch. Some people just know how to make coffee. Something genetic, maybe."

"I meant the greenhouse."

"Oh. I think the power must have cut off last night."

Larry left Wayne and rushed to the greenhouse. He saw Agnes and his mother standing mute as his father was moving from table to table and checking plant after plant. Finally he straightened up, his face looking years older and his body as wilted as his spirit. "They're dead. I don't think I can save any of them."

"What happened?" Larry asked.

"The alarm didn't go off. It froze in here and the alarm didn't sound in the house."

"How could that happen?"

His father shook his head. "I don't know. The alarm's working now."

"You're kidding."

"And the heat's back on."

Larry was silent for a moment. "I've got to do something. I'll be back."

Wayne was still at the table. He grinned when he saw Larry. "How are the cacti?"

"Let's talk."

Wayne settled back. "Okay."

"Not here—someplace private."

Wayne nodded. "All right—I know a place that's private."

He led Larry out of the house toward the stables. Larry recognized they were heading toward Mandarin's old stall.

"No one around here now," Wayne said. "The horse that lived here is gone."

Larry closed the door behind them. "That's what this is about, isn't it?"

Wayne looked puzzled. "I don't understand, Bro."

"The cacti freezing last night."

"When things get cold they freeze. An act of God."

"God didn't do it," Larry said.

"What do you mean?"

"Did you shut off the alarm system?"

Wayne stared at him and then smiled. "No one will ever know for sure what happened to the alarm system."

"Do you deny your involvement?"

"I don't have to deny anything." Wayne sank down on the floor and picked up some straw. "I can look around this empty stall and remember a horse I raised and loved, and how much it hurts when you lose something you love. And now maybe Dad will understand how that feels."

Larry moved closer and looked down at Wayne. "I told Dad he shouldn't have sold Mandarin. I told you I was on your side. But no more. I'm not on your side anymore.'

"Hold on, Bro," Wayne stood hurriedly. "This has nothing to do with us. Dad needed to learn a lesson."

"Years of his life were invested in those cacti, but he's invested more years of his life in us. If he knew what really happened, what do you think he'd consider his biggest loss?"

Wayne stared at Larry. "You're not going to tell him?"

"No," Larry said, "but I think you've lost more than a horse. And I'm just part of it." He left the stall, swinging open the door. Wayne stood motion-less, watching the door open fully, and then start closing again from the tension on its spring, slowly closing out the light.

Back in the greenhouse his father still looked dazed. Larry put his arm around his dad's shoulders. "That's all right, Dad, maybe we can save some of them. And we can always start a new collection. The hybrid—do you think we can save the *Melocactus-Phyllocactus* hybrid?"

Larry's mother had been standing in the green-house, living with the dread thought of what her older son might have done. Now as she watched her younger son she felt her heart lift in a sudden recog-nition. Who said miracles were always accompanied by the fanfare of trumpets? She knew that her youn-ger son was now closer to her husband than he had been any other time of his life. As for her older son, she believed with time, and patience, and words that could build a new bridge of communication, another miracle might happen. She believed in miracles.

RICHARD'S RENEWAL

I first saw Richard Lawrence at the Red Cross Center where I regularly visit about once a month. I used to go every two months to donate a pint of blood. But when I started donating platelets they told me I could safely go more often.

Pheresis is the procedure where you lie comfortably for nearly two hours while they transfer about sixty percent of your blood from the vein in one arm to the vein in the other arm, in between running it through a machine that removes the platelets. Three days later your body replenishes your own normal supply of platelets, while the ones you donated extend life to cancer patients.

Richard was a volunteer worker who spent three afternoons a week offering soda and cookies to donors in the refreshment room after the procedure. I estimated he was in his late seventies. He moved slowly as you might expect of someone his age, but he was smiling most of the time and always ready to talk.

74

Physically, he was under six feet, with a huge barrel chest that hinted at great arm strength in younger days. What caught my first major attention was his response when I asked for a Coke. He said he only served Mega-Cola. Would a "Meg" be all right?

I hadn't drunk a Meg for a long time, even though it was bottled locally. Mega-Cola is one of those regional competitors of Coke and Pepsi that have found a profitable niche in a particular area of the country, like Double-Cola in southeastern Tennessee. In fact, the local Mega-Cola bottling plant is almost the same size as the Double-Cola plant in Chattanooga.

The funny thing is, I like the taste of Meg, but I seldom remember to drink it—another example where the unceasing bombardment of advertising by national brands can wire the brain for unthinking, reflexive action that make smaller brands the inhabitants of a forgotten country.

So I drank a Meg, and Richard grinned when he told me serving Mega-Cola was a condition he gave the Red Cross when he volunteered for duty. This was loyalty extending into his retirement years. He explained he had worked for Mega-Cola for more than fifty years, starting right after graduation from high school—first as a dock worker and then a route driver and finally a bottler on the production line, where he eventually was promoted to floor supervisor.

As the months passed and I learned more of his life history, I realized that what had happened to him in 1988 could become my fourth miracle story . . .

"It happens to all men as they get older," Dr. Rankin said, settling down in a chair and picking up Richard Lawrence's chart. "Actually, you've been rather fortunate, considering your age and the number of Mega-Colas you have drunk over the years."

Richard had himself back in order now, facing the good doctor. "Wallace," he said, "I wish you'd quit harping on that."

Dr. Rankin smiled. "I know, you'll never listen to me. How many years has it been since I told you to cut down?"

"I've run through two other doctors before you who said the same thing. At least I don't smoke."

"It's not just the caffeine, you know." Dr. Rankin adjusted his glasses and stared harder at the chart. "Although that contributes to your condition. You remember your last bout with prostatitus?"

Richard squirmed. He had never felt so miserable in his life. No energy, a feeling of total misery—the equivalent of being run over by a sixteen-wheeler right before you had to play a hockey game.

Dr. Rankin went on, "The good news is that you don't have prostatitus."

Richard was relieved. "I just haven't been feeling good."

"Other things can cause that." Dr. Rankin laughed. "Maybe you haven't adjusted to the easy life. How does it feel not having to get up at five-thirty and going to work every day?"

"So you think my problem is mental?" Richard asked.

"I didn't say that." Dr. Rankin laid aside the chart. "You're in fine shape for someone who's seventy. Sure, your prostate *is* enlarged, but it feels healthy."

Richard groaned at the thought of "feel."

"But you should cut down on the soft drinks," the doctor went on, "not only for your prostate, but the sugar. You don't want to develop diabetes."

Richard nodded and stood. "Okay. Thanks, Wallace."

Dr. Rankin smiled and shook his hand. "I know you've worked for Mega-Cola all your life, but you don't have to drink Megs until you die."

As Richard left the office he looked forward to reaching the bottling plant where he could buy another Meg.

Richard pushed fifty cents into the vending machine and waited for the reluctant growl that presaged the clunk of the falling can. He reached deep into the slot and dragged out a twelve-ounce can graced with the Mega-Cola logo that was spelled out in yellow cursive against a blue background. Below it were the words: "Where Thirst Meets Fulfillment." Forty years ago the company had tried a new tag line: "The Taste That Lingers." But after a trial period the ad agency thought that translated into the image of "aftertaste," and most people had a negative reaction to the idea of an aftertaste.

Richard grinned when he saw Mitch Kelly walking toward him. He had given Mitch his first job at Mega-Cola, that was—in 1969, right. Nineteen years ago. Time flies, Richard thought, and had trouble realizing that five months already had passed since his own retirement.

He was proud of Mitch. He remembered the thin eighteen-year-old kid loaded with freckles and long sideburns, coming to him straight out of high school. He was willing to take any job, and Richard gave him one. He saw a fire in Mitch's eyes that reminded him of himself at that age.

Now as Richard shook Mitch's hand he remembered

how Mitch attended night classes at Vocational Tech, earning an associate business degree, and how proud he was when Mitch moved into the front office. After his last promotion to the position of assistant manager for total plant operations, Mitch still had a fire in his eyes.

But something else was also in his eyes as he smiled at Richard. "Good morning, Richard. Back again—"

Richard nodded, drinking from his can.

"—And still drinking Mega-Cola," Mitch added.

"Can't do without my Meg."

Mitch laughed. "How many Megs do you think you've drunk?"

"Since I began working here in 1937? You figure it out—fifty-one years times 365 days times an average of three Megs a day."

Mitch shook his head. "That's a lot of Megs. When you retired we recognized you as our longest-working employee. Maybe we should have called you our best customer, as well."

Richard smiled and looked at the distant activity where a moving line of cans was getting its whooshing downspouted allotment of carbonated fluid. "This place is like a second home to me, Mitch."

Mitch smiled and then his expression changed as he hesitated. "Richard, I need to talk to you for a minute. You have the time?"

"Sure."

"Let's go to the snack room." He nodded toward an exit to the hallway. "No one will be there now."

The snack room was carpeted with a brown diagonal pattern of contrasting shades. Round tables with six surrounding chairs were scattered around the room, with one wall covered by a variety of vending machines offering everything from aspirin and hair combs to candy, soup, and coffee. A microwave sat on a nearby table.

Mitch pressed the button for a cup of black coffee and moved slowly to the table where Richard was sitting. He sat back and let out a long breath.

"Everything okay, in the office?" Richard asked.

Mitch nodded, slowly sipping. "This coffee never gets better."

"A Meg is better," Richard said.

Mitch smiled briefly. He looked at Richard. "How's retirement?"

"Great," Richard said.

"Keeping busy?"

"Well," Richard hesitated, "you know how it is. You work at a place for fifty years; you miss it a little. And Paula is still working. So I like to come down here."

Mitch was quiet a moment, staring at his coffee. He spoke slowly. "Richard, I've been asked to tell you something. Maybe you had better not come down here so much."

Richard stared at Mitch, who continued speaking.

"You hired me, Richard, gave me my first job. You encouraged me to take classes and get a business degree. You spoke a good word for me to the guys upline."

Mitch looked directly at Richard. "You were the best boss I ever had. But some of the guys here are complaining a little. You're here so much, and everybody wants to talk to you." Mitch smiled. "You know how you always felt about work distractions."

"I hired most of these guys," Richard said.

"I know, Richard, but you're not their boss anymore."

"Did Martin complain?" Richard asked. He had recommended Martin to take his job.

Mitch shook his head. "Not Martin. Look, every-body likes you, Richard. You're probably the most ad-mired employee who's ever worked for Mega-Cola." Mitch reached out and touched his shoulder. "But Richard, maybe if you didn't come around so much?"

Richard didn't reply, and the two men sat silent.

"I know that retirement must be hard," Mitch finally added, "and I'd like you to consider something." He handed Richard a slip of paper.

"That's the name and phone number of a profes-sional counselor I think could help you."

"You think I'm sick?"

"No, but I think you'd enjoy talking to this woman. It always helps to talk to someone."

"I can talk to Paula," Richard said.

"Of course, but this woman can be totally objec-tive. She's talked to other people like you."

Richard took a final drink from his can of Mega-Cola. "I won't bother you again," he said, starting to rise.

"Richard, please—" Mitch touched his arm, "—call her and make an appointment. I've already mentioned you to her. All the cost is taken care of. Just try her—one time. Will you do that?"

"I'll—consider it," Richard said. "Thanks, Mitch." He turned and walked toward the door. Mitch sat staring at the door for a long time after Richard had passed from view. Soon people began coming into the room for their mid-morning break, the sound of their voices bouncing off the hard walls. But for Mitch the room still felt empty.

Richard walked blindly into the parking lot and moved to where he had parked under a roof overhang to keep shade on his car. He wouldn't worry about shade anymore. Fastening his seat belt, he carefully backed out his four-year-old Toyota Corolla and pointed toward the open gate. On Pickens Drive he headed west toward War Memorial Park, located two miles from downtown.

He had taken his sons there on Saturdays. They liked to watch the ducks on the man-made lake and ride the paddle-floats. Sometimes in the spring they would fly kites. And always the boys would want to sit on the steps leading up to the monument that honored those who fought in World War II.

This was when they tried to get their father to tell them about the war. The three of them would sit on the steps leading up to a level area of ground on which rested a twenty-foot-high obelisk, and Richard related some of the humorous and often ridiculous events and situations emanating from military life. But what he didn't tell them was the way fear felt when you were in a foxhole and ordered to advance against concrete bunkers and pillboxes. He didn't tell them the way death smelled.

When Richard had graduated from high school in 1937, his only concern was to get a job, save money, and marry Paula Medford a year later when she graduated. He got the job, married Paula on August 14, 1938, and their first child came on October 23, 1939. But Richard's plans as a working man, husband, and father changed radically after December 7, 1941. He enlisted in the marines and was shipped to the Pacific theater.

All he then knew about the war was that a lot of islands nobody had ever heard of had to be taken back from the Japanese. This meant a pattern of sea and air bombardment followed by amphibious landings under a hail of enemy mortar shells and machine gun bullets. Then followed close-range fighting through dense foliage, sometimes hand to hand, featuring flame throwers and hand grenades. Richard's Second Marine Division fought for nearly six months on Guadalcanal before final victory. But then on Tarawa the Second Marine Division achieved victory in only four days, yet Tarawa was the most costly battle in terms of time involved. More than one thousand Americans were killed and twenty-four hundred were wounded. All but seventeen of the forty-five hundred Japanese garrison were killed. Richard never knew how he survived both battles without serious injury.

Then after the war Richard returned home to his wife and son and job, just like millions of other veterans. His second son was born in 1947.

Richard turned on to a side street and parked near the north entrance to the grounds. He got out and walked slowly toward the obelisk. He could almost feel the hand of his four-year-old son, Elliott, tugging at his arm as they headed toward the monument. On his other side twelve-year-old Wade, growing impatient with their slow pace, would suddenly run ahead of them, causing Elliott to give chase in a futile effort to keep up. With eight years' difference in age, keeping both boys together for their park excursions lasted only until 1953. After that Wade slipped away to his own interests.

Funny thing about Paula—she never would come with them to the park. She always said that father and sons should have a little time alone with each other, and Saturday morning was their time.

Richard now sat on the third step up, in the same place as he had with the boys. The obelisk was still pointing toward eternity. The words of honor were still inscribed at the base of the monument. The memories of the war, of his children, of his many years on the job—they were there, but he no longer felt close to any of them. He had never felt more alone in his life.

His service buddies—most of them dead. His children grown up and gone. His wife with her own job and circle of friends. His career was over. What was left? What was the point of any of it? He was in a way, a relic, not needed, not wanted.

He leaned back on the step and closed his eyes.

He had really been something, coming out of high school crazy in love with a driving ambition to find a job, get married, and start a family. Those were the important things to anyone living through the depression.

At Mega-Cola he was soon promoted from the dock, thoroughly determined to be the top route driver in customer loyalty and sales.

Those days drinks were in bottles, not cans, and his job was to haul out a truck of full cases and bring back a load of empty bottles. In mid-afternoon when he pulled into the plant the dock crew would help him unload the empties, sort the bottles according to shape—cola or fruit drink—then stack the sorted empty cases on stacks that could be moved to the bottling section for reuse.

Richard liked to work fast during the day so he would be one of the first drivers back and not have to wait in line to check his cash receipts against deliveries. This let him get home earlier.

Another way to speed up the process was to challenge the dock crew. He made games of unloading and stacking cases. He could throw full cases around as easily as some could handle empty cases. The crew liked to make wagers on his strength.

Old timers would challenge any new worker to sling

a full case of Mega-Cola as high as he could on the stack. Another test was to ask the newcomer to hook the tips of his fingers over the railing of a sliding exit door and chin himself. Usually three, maybe four times, was all straining muscles could achieve. So they would then bring forth this chunky guy two inches under six feet and ask the newcomer questions:

How high could this guy sling a full case? Seven, eight, nine feet? How about ten feet? The usual response—no way, and bets were made.

Then about the chin-ups. How many? Ten, fifteen, twenty? How about thirty? Again the response—no way. More bets made. And the newcomer suddenly with lighter pockets now became someone who looked forward to the next newcomer.

Richard slowly rose and then moved around the obelisk. He stopped and looked up at the tip. The reporter had been right. When Richard was a senior an AP reporter visited the school as assembly speaker. The reporter had just finished an assignment in Germany. He spoke of the armed buildup in Germany, the tone of Hitler's speeches and how he unilaterally had repudiated the war-guilt clause of the Versailles Treaty. Then he said that the pacifist sentiment so widespread in Great Britain and the U.S. was wrong. Appeasing Hitler would only bring about a war. And then at the end of his speech, he had pointed to the student body, moving his arm over the entire assembly, and warned them that every male student—even the freshmen—would soon be fighting in a war against Germany.

Back in his car Richard looked at the slip of paper that Mitch had given him. "Cynthia Everhart . . . Counseling." Simple enough, he thought. Counseling about what? Anything, everything? Or about nothing—which is all some people ever talk about. Mitch had already talked to her. The day was still young. Why not give her a call?

He used a pay phone in front of the Corner Market, right across the street from the park.

"Hello?" The voice was soft and musical.

Richard hesitated. "Cynthia Everhart?"

"Yes."

"I believe Mitch Kelly talked to you about me."

A moment's pause. "Your name?"

"Richard Lawrence."

"Yes, he did."

Richard cleared his throat. "Mitch said he thought I might talk to you."

"I would enjoy that," she said.

Richard was revising his feelings. Now he wanted to talk to her—not so much for himself, but to see what kind of woman went with that fantastic voice. After all, he was only seventy.

"May I make an appointment?" he asked.

"I have time now," she said, "not for a long session, but we could meet and get to know each other."

Richard was definitely looking forward to this meeting more than the one he had with Dr. Rankin. He got her address and said he'd be there in less than thirty minutes.

Cynthia Everhart's office was on the eighth floor of the Crestview Building, a prestige address filled with architects, insurance agents, and lawyers. A middle-aged woman was seated at the receptionist's desk in the outer office. Richard gave her his name and she immediately announced him to Cynthia.

Her office was done in a Mediterranean style, modern furniture with extremely simple design. The carpet and walls blended together with warm pastel shades.

Two chairs were near each other in one corner, away from her desk. That's where she invited him to sit.

"Would you like some coffee?" she asked.

"No, thanks."

She grinned. "A Meg?"

He shook his head.

"Mitch told me how loyal you are to Mega-Cola. He also said you worked there for more than fifty years?"

"That's right. Since 1938—of course, that counts the years I spent in the war."

She smiled. "How extraordinary."

Richard was having trouble putting the woman with the voice. She looked fifty, an attractive fifty with close-cropped gray hair framing a rather square-shaped face, but her voice was youthful and sang with the promise of intimate secrets.

They talked for a while about his work. He told her about his accident in 1952 when a tractor-trailer rig sideswiped his truck while trying to pass in a heavy rain, causing Richard's truck to tumble down a deep ditch and land hard on its side. He came out of the wreck with a problem back, and the company did not want him to drive anymore. After therapy he was transferred to the bottling plant.

Richard grew more enthusiastic as he recounted his feelings in the new job. He made a friend of every piece of equipment, learning the way every moving part fit together and should sound during operation. He explained he developed a kind of sixth sense for predicting where breakdowns might occur. And when he was made supervisor it seemed he had been pointed toward this job all his life.

Cynthia asked him how he felt about his retirement, and he described the big dinner held in his honor, and how his bosses and co-workers scalded him with jokes and lavished him with testimonials. The plant manager gave him a plaque, and the president of Mega-Cola presented him with a gold watch that had been inscribed on back: "Richard Lawrence, for 51 years a Mega-employee."

He told how after the dinner a lot of his co-workers bunched around him and made comments about his now having lots of time to fish, play golf, watch TV, and lie in the hammock. They voiced their pleasure that a man who had worked so hard for so many years could now reap the rewards of an easy life.

"Do you still see your friends?" she asked.

"I have been. At work—I've been visiting them a lot." he hesitated. "But I won't be, not so much. Not anymore."

"What about your friends away from work?"

"I don't have many friends," he said. "I worked long hours for a lot of years. Didn't have a chance to meet many people away from work."

"Maybe it would help to make new friends."

Richard grinned. "How would I do that? At my age?"

"Church, or clubs?" she suggested.

He shook his head. "Church wasn't for me. And I didn't have any time for clubs."

Cynthia smiled. "What do you consider your favorite recreation?"

He thought a moment. "I don't know." Then his face suddenly lit up with a big grin. "I guess it would be drinking Mega-Cola."

She looked at him quizzically.

"I'm serious," he said. "My doctor is trying to get me to stop drinking them, but I've lived to be seventy and they haven't hurt me. By now they're just part of my life."

"That's interesting, Mr. Lawrence. But maybe you'll decide that you should change your life a little." She looked closely at him. "Tell me one more thing. Looking at your life right now, how do you feel about your retirement?"

Richard shuffled in his chair. "I worked a lot of years," he said.

She nodded.

"And I was seventy. It was time."

She nodded again. "A lot of people retire much earlier than you. But how do you *feel* about not working?"

"I feel good."

She smiled. "Why don't we set up another appointment?"

Why not?—he told himself. He had enjoyed himself. And she surely was a good listener.

They made an appointment for the following Tuesday, and Richard got on the elevator to take him to the fifth floor of the parking garage. All the places on lower floors had been filled when he arrived.

A woman was standing in the elevator. She looked about thirty-two and had obviously been crying. She smiled briefly at him and looked down at her purse. Her hair was done in one of those kinky, frizzy styles, and her face was highlighted by a mole strategically placed about one inch to the left of her mouth and a half inch up. The hallowed beauty mark of famous silent screen sirens.

Richard thought at first it was artificial, but on closer and unobtrusive inspection he saw it was real. She was aware of his curiosity and used her handkerchief, smiling at him.

"Hay fever," she said, but her lower lip trembled and made the smile a lie.

The elevator stopped and a middle-aged woman in a gray coat stepped in. "Oh!" she exclaimed as the car started up. She looked sheepish. "I thought this was going down."

Richard smiled at her, but glanced at the young woman. She was busy with the handkerchief again and with finality put the handkerchief into her purse and straightened up, making a supreme effort at self-composure. Richard had seen a lot of troubled people in his seventy years. Employees at work, marines in combat. In war he had seen faces of fear and anxiety, faces expressing the agony of receiving a Dear John letter, frozen faces watching waves of Japanese soldiers making a suicide charge with fixed bayonets.

Here was a woman highly distraught, facing her own bayonet charge.

The car stopped at the fifth floor. The middle-aged woman backed up to let the young woman and Richard pass. Outside many of the cars had left the floor. Richard's car was halfway to the end, and he found himself walking beside the woman. She was looking down as she walked. Nearing his car he said, "I hope your hay fever gets better."

Again that quick smile as she moved on. Suddenly she stopped, staring ahead. "Randy—no!" she exclaimed, and began running toward the far end.

Richard saw in the distance a man leaning over the driver's door of a red sedan. It looked like the man was using a coat hanger to break into the car. The woman reached him and they began arguing. The man yelled something and grabbed the woman's purse, tearing it open. The woman was pulling at his arm. Richard couldn't hear their words distinctly. The man suddenly pushed her away violently and she stumbled backward and fell.

Richard began walking rapidly toward them. He wanted to run, but he didn't want to be panting and out of breath when he got there. The woman staggered up, and now Richard could make out the words.

"I warned you not to take the car!"

"It's my car, Randy. I paid for it."

"You made the down payment." He threw the purse at her feet, holding the keys. "But it's my car and I'm taking it!" He started to get into the car.

"Just a minute," Richard said. The man looked at him for the first time. "I think you owe this woman an apology."

"Who are you?" the man asked.

"A human being," Richard answered, "which seems to be more than what I'm looking at."

The man stared, and then looked at the woman, "Who's this old man—your granddad?"

"I'm old enough to spank unruly grandchildren," Richard said.

The man stepped away from the car, slamming the door behind him. The woman touched Richard's arm. "Please, let him go—"

"Listen to her," the man said.

"I will," Richard said, "but first, an apology, and then give her the keys."

The man grinned. "You think you can make me?"

"What I can do might surprise you."

The man stopped smiling. His hand reached in a pocket and came out, a blade flicked open and held waist high.

Richard's memory flashed to a moonlit night on Tarawa. They had finished mopping up the last Japanese resistance, and were trying any way they could to numb the guilt of surviving while so many who had fought next to them had died.

The guys in Richard's platoon were shooting craps. Richard was winning and on a roll when he was suddenly challenged by Ted Carter as using loaded dice. Richard knew he was grieving over his best buddy, who had taken a bullet in the chest. He used mollifying words but the next instant Ted was holding an open knife. Other guys quickly grabbed him and then Ted dropped the knife and began crying like a baby.

This man didn't look like he was going to cry. He held the knife in front of him and stepped toward Richard, trying to bluff him.

"Go on. Get away," the man muttered. "Get out of here. This is none of your business. She can't divorce me and think she can take my car—"

Richard feinted a step forward and the man jabbed in the air with his knife. Richard grabbed his wrist quickly with both hands and twisted, but the man didn't drop the knife. Richard jammed his heel on the man's left foot. The man yelled and jerked back, but still held the knife. His face looked dazed. He couldn't believe this old guy could be so strong. Now his face set in a more serious expression, and he tried to bring his knife down lower to point toward Richard's chest.

Richard grunted. Twenty years ago he would have had the knife and the man would have been groaning on the pavement. He tried to knee the man's groin, but missed the target. The man doubled over slightly, and seemed to muster all his strength to jerk the knife toward Richard. But Richard still held onto the man's wrist, forcing the knife point away from him.

"Damn you!" the man yelled with one final jerk, and the knife blade entered the right side of his neck. His expression changed, his eyes staring at Richard in stunned disbelief. He dropped the knife and grabbed his throat, then stared at his hand covered with blood.

His eyes glazed as Richard quickly grabbed him and pressed his hand against the man's neck. "We've got to get him to the hospital."

The man was passing out as Richard struggled with him to get him into the woman's car. He kept his hand pressed hard against the man's neck all the way to the Emergency Room of the Harding Road Hospital.

The attending physician muttered, "Carotid," before moving him into a room off the hallway. Then came questions and paperwork, and the fact the hospital would notify the police since this was a knife wound.

Richard learned the man was Randolph Satterfield, a mobile home salesman, and his wife was Lily, who didn't know he used drugs when she married him. She had cried herself out by the time a doctor appeared.

"He's lost a lot of blood but he's stable. You know his blood type?"

"No," Lily said.

"That's all right. We're giving him O negative now, which is compatible with all types."

"Do you need more blood?" Richard asked.

The doctor nodded. "The Red Cross Center always needs blood—all types, but O negative is the one that is safe to transfuse to any other blood type."

"I'm O negative," Richard said.

"Congratulations," the doctor smiled. "you're in the six percent of the population who have that type. The Red Cross Center would like to see you."

After Richard and Lily talked to the police, answering detailed questions and leaving his name for any more police followup, Richard immediately went to the Red Cross Center. It had been years since he had donated blood, and he felt a little guilty.

When they were taking his blood he thought back on what the counselor had said, that maybe he ought to change his life. Some changes now were forced on him, like not going to the plant every day and seeing old friends. So he needed to make new friends, like Lily. He had enjoyed talking to her, even under the circumstances. And heaven help him, he had enjoyed the fight—looking back on it. He felt like he could still function, could do something worthwhile. But he had to take the initiative.

Maybe that's what made people feel old, just sitting back and waiting. Perhaps old age is resigning yourself to watching others live.

Later, in the Red Cross refreshment room, he sat at a table filled with various crackers and cookies. A woman not much younger than himself asked him what he wanted to drink, a Coke or orange juice? He could do what she was doing, he thought—a good way to meet new and interesting people. Wouldn't take much of his time, maybe a few days a week. And the sign in the hall said they wanted volunteers.

He smiled to himself. One thing, though—after he worked with them long enough to get a little pull, he'd try to make Mega-Cola the cola offered.

But now as he sat looking at the woman offering him a drink, he thought of his doctor who wanted him to cut way down on Megs. Yes, he needed a life change.

Richard decided to make the grand gesture. For anyone wanting a cola the best choice would always be Mega-Cola. But for him, now, facing the rest of his life . . .

He spoke the earth-shattering words. "I'd like some orange juice."

DOUG'S DILEMMA

I started going to Fitness World after my bath-
room scales went tilt one morning right before I
launched into my usual shaving ablutions.
"Tilt" for me was ten pounds above my fighting
weight. I had been aware of the spiraling en-
hancement of bloat, but a pound at a time
makes awareness a victim of creeping gradual-
ism. Ten pounds, however, shouts for action.

Fitness World was one of the newest empori-
ums of energy expenditure in our city, occupying
one of the remodeled historic waterfront buildings
downtown. It was within walking distance of the
newspaper, and I found it convenient as well as
beneficial to select exercise as my lunch menu
item of choice.

Doug Mangrum was part owner of Fitness
World, and a better representative of the body
exemplar could never be found. Think of him
not as a modern Mr. Olympia with muscles
about to burst open the skin. Rather, think of the
Greek ideal of an Olympic athlete as personi-
fied in the classical statues of antiquity.

On top of that, he was a friendly guy, very

94

*open in selling his facility without the hype you
sometimes get from physical gurus on TV. I later
learned he was also on TV, an early Saturday-
morning exercise program that ran on a local
independent station.*

*He gave me a tour of the place, told me that
losing ten pounds should be no problem, and I
signed up.*

*He was right about losing the ten pounds,
which took me two months. But I was glad to
hang around beyond that because I liked what
regular exercise did to my body. I never expected to look like Doug, though. Not that I
would have minded, seeing the way that beautiful women seemed to prolong their gazes in his
direction.*

*We were close in age, and often found our-
selves sitting at a table in the refreshment area
downing a bottle of orange or apple juice, and
sharing life experiences. Eventually he told me
of an earlier time when he worked at a different
fitness center, and I realized I had found my fifth
miracle story . . .*

When Doug entered the Bunny Box on a Thursday
spring morning the first thing he saw was a girl,
about eighteen, doing a stretching gyration around a
vertical brass post that reached from floor to ceiling
on the platform. He recognized her as one of the locals who occasionally was allowed to do a solo routine. She wasn't in Linda's class.

Linda was definitely the pick of the current litter of
imports. With her long flowing brown hair coming
down to her waist, and the longest legs this side of a

stilted clown, she had a spectacular act as she found many ways of wrapping herself around the pole.

On his way back to Lou's office Doug saw the usual two battle tanks that always stayed close to Lou. They were at a table playing gin rummy, both wearing string ties—a testimony of Lou's devotion to country music. He always insisted his "protection engineers" reflect his own sense of sartorial style.

"Hey, Adonis," one guy called. "Where you going?"

"To see Lou," Doug said.

"Hold on." He stood up and Doug marveled again at how big Al "Red Dog" Eggers was. At least six-six, with shoulders as massive as the burial graves of the Tennessee mound builders. Doug had never liked Al, and now watched the crooked smile on his face spread as he got nearer.

"You've got to be kidding," Doug said.

"Sorry, pal," Al muttered as he patted Doug down. "That's my job."

"I work for Lou, too."

"Yeah," Al said, "oiling springs on squeaking beds."

The guy at the table laughed. "No, Al—Adonis don't use beds anymore with the girls. He's gotten more creative."

Doug stepped back from Al. He had a strong desire to send the back edge of his right hand into Al's throat. Al's eyes squinted.

"You through?" Doug asked.

"Yeah."

"My turn," Doug said, reaching out to pat the front of Al's coat. Suddenly his hand darted inside the coat and an instant later he was holding a thirty-eight special pointing straight at Al's chest.

"You guys are real comedians," Doug said, "but take your act somewhere else. Try that routine again and I'll jam this gun up your nose and tickle your left eyeball."

Al stared at him, and Doug could feel the rage coming at him in waves.

"Catch," Doug said, tossing the gun.

Al fumbled at it and sputtered, "You may think you're the fair-haired boy, but wait until you make a mistake." Then more calmly he grinned as he holstered the gun. "I'm going to enjoy that."

"Why don't you find a water hydrant and relieve yourself?" Doug said, and walked on to Lou's office. When he tapped on the door Lou sang out to come in.

"Doug, what brings you here this time of day?" Lou was working over some papers.

"A special request, but now I've got another request. I'd like you to tell Red Dog to quit pushing me."

"What happened?"

"He just frisked me. I don't like it."

Lou straightened up. "He shouldn't have done that."

"I don't want him doing it again."

"I'll talk to him."

"He's always riding me."

"He just resents your success with the ladies," Lou grinned. "I don't think he's had much success lately. Sit down, Doug."

Doug sat. "I won't take much of your time, Lou. It's about Linda."

Lou smiled and leaned back in his deep-cushioned black leather chair and propped his feet on the desk.

"What about Linda?"

"She's the best dancer you've got," Doug said.

Lou nodded, still smiling. "Right."

"How about letting her stay on a couple more weeks?"

Lou smirked. "Haven't got enough of her yet?"

Doug never liked to hear that kind of talk—the inference being that he was some kind of sex machine. From the goons—he could expect it. He didn't appreciate Lou always making cracks.

"I like Linda a lot."

"Sure, you do. You like a lot of women. And I'm not knocking it. If I looked like you do I'd run ads in the paper and charge women fees for service."

Doug tightened his jaw. He'd be glad when he could wave good-bye to Lou, his goons, and his other assorted associates.

"How about it—letting Linda stay?" Doug asked.

Lou hesitated a moment. "Did Linda put you up to this?"

"My idea," Doug said. "At least keep her until the Detroit girls get here."

Lou shook his head. "Sorry, Doug. Harry's expecting her in Kansas City. She leaves tomorrow."

"Thanks, anyway," Doug said drily.

Lou grinned broadly. "At least you've got tonight. Make it one she'll never forget."

Doug stood to leave. Lou's words stopped him. "Anyone ever call you an addict?"

"What kind of addict?"

"You have to ask?"

"I'm no addict," Doug said.

"I don't mean drugs or liquor. But you can't get enough of women, can you?"

"You think I'm addicted to sex?"

"Aren't you?"

"Of course not."

"How many women have you had in the last month?"

Doug frowned. "So long, Lou." He turned away.

"Hey—hold on." Lou straightened in his chair. "Don't go away mad. I'm just envious."

"I need to get back."

"You're a good boy, Doug. I made a smart move hiring you and letting you run the Palace Physique. Women enrollments have increased sixty-two percent in the last six months. They like what they see at the Palace, and the personal attention you give." Lou grinned broadly. "Especially the personal attention. Just be careful of angry husbands. I don't want any lawsuits."

Doug turned and walked toward the door.

Lou called out, "You're going to like the Detroit crop."

When Doug pulled out of the parking lot and made his way through the familiar streets to the Palace Physique, instinct took over and his conscious mind wandered over the path that had led to his involvement with Lou Kessler. Not the kind of guy he would have approached for employment. For one thing, Lou's associates weren't Sunday-school teachers. Doug didn't see them much because they lived in other cities. And Doug didn't want to know anything else about them. Just looking at them was enough. Expensive suits and lip hair and jewelry that hadn't come from Super Cash Pawn and Jewelry. And the way they shipped the dancers around bothered him.

Lou kept a string of local girls on his payroll—around forty—most part time. A few locals were given a chance to perform. But most were for decoration and easing cash out of the customers' pockets.

The real performers—the headliners—were imported, staying two weeks or a month and then moving to the next city.

So who runs an operation where girls are sent all over the country? Doug could guess, and he didn't want to pry deeper.

He remembered the way his dad had talked about the time a national union had organized the local truck drivers. His father drove for Bountiful Foods, and he described how outside guys had come in with intimidation and muscle. After that anything that smelled of a mob connection had made his dad furious.

Now Doug could smell fumes of his own. But he was optimistic—if he and Cindy could work out their deal with Quentin Reese, he would be free and clear of Lou Kessler.

The Palace Physique had once been called Weyman's Gym. That's when Doug had started working. Fresh out of college with a degree in physical education, Doug had sent his resume to every fitness center in the city. He wanted to stay in his hometown. Old Cliff Weyman was the first to respond.

He was nearing retirement, but he still spent time working out every day. In the interview he had asked Doug what he thought should comprise a good facility. Doug swallowed, and with a slew of courses on exercise science lifetime fitness, and weight training behind him, launched into a description of the variety of programs required to meet all sorts of fitness needs in today's world. In general terms he spoke of how a modern facility should be more than a gym, but offer modern fitness equipment systems that could be used to create personalized training programs that were administered by a knowledgeable staff. He felt later that he had gotten carried away, but Cliff had only smiled at his enthusiasm, and within a week Doug had a job.

Cindy Byars was already working there. She was two years older than he, and after meeting her, Doug placed her in the category of potential close friend, platonic.

Not that she wasn't physically attractive. She was, but she reminded Doug of his younger sister. The same light brown hair. Figure good but not outstanding. Fine skin, quick smile. She seemed unassuming, without pretension, someone he could relate to in an open, honest way without any hidden agenda or sexual tension. A rarity, because Doug had no other woman friend like that.

His relationship with girls had been an almost continuous parade of triumphant gratification since the eighth grade. He had always been comfortable around girls, with an easy manner that kept him a little remote, making girls sense in him a kind of challenge. If this gave him an edge over other guys, he never tried to analyze it. He did nothing deliberately as a way to manipulate anyone, which may have been another secret of his success with women.

Doug had no ethical absolutes that would dampen his effort to seek sexual gratification. If a woman were agreeable and desired a romantic outcome, Doug saw nothing wrong in the fulfillment of that goal.

In fact, by this time in his life he accepted the whole process of man and woman getting together as no more unnatural than wearing shoes. Every attractive woman he met he automatically evaluated in terms of sexual appeal, judging from the obvious circumstances whether to make a further overture.

And those circumstances were important to Doug.

He never encouraged any woman who was married, recently widowed or divorced, or any single woman where he sensed some kind of emotional instability that might create an obsessive attachment (although this judgment could be tricky). But with the other single women, if they appealed to him and he sensed a like response, it was tickets for two hopefully on a train ride to the ramparts of paradise.

But with Cindy the ticket had been only for a ride of mutually shared interest in the welfare of Weyman's Gym. Within two years Weyman had developed cancer of the liver, and suddenly he was faced with medical bills—only partially covered by his insurance—and the desire to leave his wife with as much financial help as possible.

He put Weyman's Gym up for sale, and responses were disappointing. Except—there was one offer far better than the rest, from the owner and operator of the Bunny Box.

Weyman didn't like Lou Kessler. He didn't like Kessler's business, and didn't want his place to end up in Kessler's hands. He was almost in tears when he announced to Doug and Cindy his decision to sell to Kessler.

"I don't know why he wants the place," Weyman said.

"You've got a good name, Cliff," Doug suggested. "If I owned the Bunny Box I wouldn't mind owning something else that sounded more respectable."

"He wants you two to stay on," Weyman added, "even said he'd increase your salaries." Weyman reached out and took hold of both Cindy's and Doug's hands. "I'm sorry. But I need to make the best deal I can."

At first Doug and Cindy had no problems with the

new ownership. Lou was solicitous about their feelings, and followed their advice in improving and remodeling the facility. He even secured a weekly fitness program for Doug on a local independent TV station. Lou explained that one of the partners owning the station owed him a favor.

The first rumble of discontent came with the name change. Both Doug and Cindy disliked "Palace Physique."

"People don't exercise in a palace," Cindy said. "They eat rich food and drink themselves into a stupor in a palace."

Lou smiled and said the new name had "class."

Later Cindy said to Doug, "He wants a name with class when he owns the 'Bunny Box'?"

"I think we'd better work toward finding a place where we can start our own class," Doug commented.

Doug forced himself to quit walking the pathway of reverie when he pulled into the parking lot of the Palace Physique. Almost all of the parking places were full. A lot of women came on Thursday morning for the class that Cindy led in the large aerobics room. This room contained a wood floor covered by a synthetic surface that allowed a cushioning effect to minimize the shin splints and other bone and ligament injuries sometimes caused by the vigorous routines. Cindy was winding up with the slow music that accompanied the relaxing and stretching postures. Soon one hundred and fifty women were on their way to the showers, home, or to other activities in the building.

Cindy smiled a greeting. "Quentin called, he'd like us to meet him at the waterfront. I told him eleven."

Doug nodded, and led her into his office. "You think he's ready to make a deal?"

She nodded. "He sounded like it."

Doug grinned. He and Quentin had been talking for more than three months. Quentin was a real estate developer who owned or controlled almost three city blocks of property fronting the river that bounded the north side of downtown. It was a historic section of run-down buildings that was now in the process of renovation. Clients were few at this point, and Quentin was always trying to encourage more businesses to fill his buildings and hopefully build momentum to make the riverfront a popular hub of downtown activity.

When Doug and Cindy arrived at the old building that once had been a shipping warehouse for riverbound traffic, he felt the same surge of excitement that always brought a tingle when he thought of having his own place. He and Cindy would be partners—putting up all their savings. But what they needed was another partner with deeper pockets, and Quentin seemed an ideal prospect.

Quentin was inside with another man. Doug and Cindy had been in this building many times and visualized the possible arrangements of the facilities and equipment. They knew they would not be able to have as much space as they would like, but felt they would be able to give the public a quality operation.

Quentin Reese was in his early fifties, a shade over five feet six inches, with a stomach that had too readily shaped itself to appease a voracious appetite. When he and Doug had first begun talking about a possible deal, Quentin admitted that his personal interest in a fitness establishment might stem from more than an objective business evaluation. Later in their discussions it became obvious that Quentin not only was willing to offer a good financial arrangement on the property, he might be interested in investing as a partner.

Now he introduced Doug and Cindy to Paul Friedman, slim and in his early forties.

"Paul is thinking about opening a health food restaurant, maybe next door. He likes the waterfront idea, but he also likes the idea of being next to a fitness center. I wanted him to meet you guys and look over your space as well as what he might occupy."

As they talked, Doug was happy to see that Paul seemed to reflect at least a guarded optimism. When they were breaking up Quentin tapped his shoulder and said, "Now we have another reason to work out a deal. I'll get back with you shortly and see if we can pin something down."

A week went by without any more contact from Quentin, so Doug was a little depressed when he pulled into the parking lot of the Bunny Box. Lou had called him to come over and meet the new girls from Detroit. As he got out of his car he saw another car drive in—a red Miata. Then a girl got out who made him stop walking.

He knew it had to be one of the new girls, no one local. She had red hair, closely cropped. She was wearing black pumps, mid-thigh tight red shorts, a chopped-off red blouse that left her stomach bare as well as her shoulders and arms.

Her muscles were cut and ripped to show every defining aspect of their texture and sinew as they pressed hard against the skin. Here was a woman who seriously worked out with weights. Many beautiful women have the soft muscle tone that implies pliant submission, but this woman looked like she could subdue a platoon of marines.

But her muscle tone was not the only unusual thing

about her. As he got closer to her he saw she had slanted eyes, looking almost Oriental except for hair and height, which was around five feet ten inches. The expression on her face seemed to mock him as he got still closer.

"Are you one of the girls from Detroit?" he asked.

She nodded and he stuck out his hand. "Hello," he smiled. "I'm Doug Mangrum."

Her mocking voice matched her expression. "Am I supposed to be impressed?" she asked, taking his hand.

"I manage the Palace Physique." Her grip was firm.

"Good for you," she said. "I'm Cat Chandu."

Doug swallowed hard, trying to keep his hand from being crushed. "Lou owns the Palace," he muttered.

She nodded and dropped his hand. He kept staring at her.

"You like what you see?" she asked. "You're not bad-looking, yourself."

Doug felt himself blushing. It had been many years since he didn't know what to say to a woman.

"You have a nice car," he stammered.

"They always furnish me with a nice car," she said.

Doug had never known Lou to furnish any girl with a car.

"If you're through staring," she said, "I need to go to the club."

"So do I," was all he managed to say. Now, he thought wryly, if only I can walk beside her without falling on my face.

Inside the club Doug moved immediately toward Lou's office. He glanced back and saw her watching him, a faint smile still on her lips as she stepped up on the platform. Then he waved at Red Dog as he passed the gin rummy table without incident. As he neared Lou's office he felt the memory of Linda receding from him like a fading dream.

Doug knocked on the door and opened it to Lou's expansive greeting. "Doug—come in, come in."

"Hello, Lou."

"Did you see any of the girls out front?"

Doug nodded. "I met one."

"The others will be out. They're in the dressing room." Lou grinned. "What did you think?"

"The one I saw wasn't bad."

"Which one?"

"The redhead."

Lou grinned. "She tell you her name?"

Doug nodded.

Lou laughed. "Isn't her name a gas? Cat Chandu. She's either going to be the biggest hit we've had or the biggest flop."

"Why do you say that?"

"Her muscles. She's not to my taste, you understand, but Benny said she went over big in Detroit and I should give her a chance here. Had to rent her a car." Lou gave him a sly look. "You like her?"

Doug was noncommittal. "I said she wasn't bad."

"She doesn't look like Linda."

Doug spread his arms. "Look, Linda was great. But Cat looks fine, too."

"Okay, Mr. Pulchritude Connoisseur, I want you to be more active"—he cleared his throat—"I mean, more active in a physical educational kind of way, with this group of girls. I'm starting a new policy."

"What policy?"

"All the out-of-town girls are going to have to work out at the Palace while they're here."

Doug grinned. "What if they don't want to?"

"They have to. That will be part of the terms of their employment." Lou stood and moved over to the wall and pointed to a color photo of a woman wearing strategically placed feathers as she slouched on a straight wooden chair.

"This was my favorite all-time dancer. She called herself Carole Coolips, but watching her act you knew a better name would have been Hedda Hotblood. I started sweating before the first feather hit the floor. And beautiful—a slender Venus de Milo with arms intact. I lost contact with her years ago after she worked with me in Minneapolis. I heard she got married."

He moved to the window and looked out. "She came by yesterday. Not married anymore. She wanted a job, not dancing—she had no illusions about that. But a job, maybe a cashier, or hostess." Lou turned to face Doug.

"She's too far over the hill. She doesn't look good enough even for a job out front somewhere. Looks can go fast, you know—if you don't take care of yourself—and when they're gone you can't get them back. I don't like heavy muscles on women, but let me tell you, most of the dancers who come in here are too soft. So while they're here, I'm going to make sure they learn a little something about keeping themselves in shape."

Doug stared at him. This didn't sound like Lou Kessler.

"I sure hated to see Carole like that," Lou said.

"I'm sorry about Carole," Doug said.

Lou smiled and slapped him on the back. "Hey, I

gave her a job. In the kitchen. She learned to cook while she was married. And if Harper doesn't want her help with the food, she can wash dishes."

He motioned to Doug and moved toward the door. "Let's go meet the girls."

Four other girls had joined Cat Chandu on the stage area. Each of them wore a distinct costume that made no effort to keep secret any physical attribute.

"Okay, girls," Lou said, "let me introduce you to Doug Mangrum. He runs a place I own called the Palace Physique." He gestured to Cat.

"You said you met Cat—Cat Chandu." Cat still wore her sardonic expression and nodded.

Doug nodded back at her.

"And this is Sandra Santini." A brunette with kinky hair smiled.

"Dawn Dearheart." A light blond with a pixie face.

"This is Lisa Love." A black woman with piercing eyes.

"And finally, Angel Allgood." By the way Lou looked at her Doug had no doubt who would be the favored employee.

"Now girls, you're going to see a lot of this man," Lou said, "and not as a customer. You're going to be his customers."

Cat spoke slowly. "I may not like what he is selling."

Lou said, "I haven't seen a woman yet who doesn't like what he sells."

Cat shrugged.

"Doug, explain about the Palace," Lou said.

"You're all dancers," Doug began, "so you know how important it is to keep in shape. But beyond how you look, your condition depends upon your aerobic fitness. We have some machines at the Palace that

will help you with that. We can also create better
muscle tone. And if some of you want to work on a
particular aspect of fitness, we'll personalize a program."

Cat drawled, "Do you think you could personalize
a program for me?" Her voice carried a meaning as
subtle as a neon billboard.

Doug's mouth felt dry. "I'll give you my personal
attention."

She nodded. "Good."

Her mocking smile carried a challenge he felt was
aimed straight at him—the challenge, if he's man
enough, to try and breach an impregnable castle that
stands supremely confident of its invincibility.

Doug liked a challenge.

"And ladies," Lou said, "while you're working for
me I expect each of you to visit the Palace Physique
at least three times a week. Doug will work with you
on your schedule and program of exercises."

When Doug told Cindy about the five Detroit girls
coming to the Palace for working out, she bristled.

"Lou has never sent any girls before."

"He called it a new policy."

"I don't like any of the Bunny Box girls coming
here."

"We can't keep them away," Doug said. "Lou does
own this place."

"But up until now both operations have been kept
separate."

"They're still separate," Doug smiled. "Lighten
up, partner. Exercise is for everyone, right? Anyway,
aren't we like a doctor?—have to serve everyone."

Cindy sniffed, "I'll be glad when we can get away
from Lou Kessler."

Cindy's attitude didn't improve when the girls arrived at the Palace. Doug could see her jaw harden as she tried to be polite. She volunteered to take the girls through the building and explain the equipment.

"I'll let Mr. Mangrum show me around," Cat said. Cindy's jaw took on a Mount Rushmore aspect. The other girls followed her as Cat assumed a wide-eyed look.

"I want to do that," she said, hurrying over to do a weight bench and lying down. She lifted up the barbell that was suspended above her and let it down on her more than ample chest. Then up, and her arm muscles jutted out like sharks in a trawling net. "Is breathing important?" she asked.

"Yes."

"Check to see if I breathe right," she said, pointing to her bare stomach. "Put your hand here."

She hoisted the barbell again. She was breathing deeply. Doug hesitated. He saw Cindy watching him from across the room. He shrugged, and placed his hand on Cat's flat, very hard stomach. She breathed, and he felt her abdominals roll under her skin as she repeated the press a number of times. Oh, yes, he thought, she knew how to breathe. But he was having trouble.

At the end of a very comprehensive workout—it was obvious that Cat was familiar with all the equipment—she whispered that she wanted him to be at the club tonight.

The rest of the day Cindy seemed a little cool. If he didn't know better he would have thought that she was steamed about Cat. But, of course, that didn't make any sense. Cindy knew he liked women, and she was his platonic pal.

The acts that night unreeled with a homogeneity of bare flesh. The drums pounded, the spotlights strobed on cue, and the music crescendoed in a final climax of artificial passion. The customers vented loud encouragement. These girls from Detroit were something!

But Doug was waiting for one act. He was not disappointed. Cat appeared in billowing wisps of sheer pastel materials. She was carrying a closed basket, and set it down in the middle of the stage. To the gradually ascending beat of drums she began to dance, circling the basket. Salome with her veils, contorting herself in time to the music. A bare arm showing. A glimpse of thigh. One veil falls. Then another. And always on her face an intensity of mockery. More veils dropped, and as the music became its most frenzied she faced the audience and with one final gesture she stood revealed, every muscle quivering in an ecstasy of wild abandon, and then as the audience quit breathing she opened the basket and pulled out a bloody severed head, holding it outstreched with a quivering arm as the music crashed to its end and the spotlight blinked off. Then erupted the roar of an audience transfixed by the fantasy of blended sadism and sex.

Later, fully dressed, Cat came to Doug's table. The challenging mockery was still in her eyes. She passed him a key and told him to go to Room 523 of the Medford Hotel. She would join him by 3:00 a.m.

"But only come," she whispered, "if you think you're man enough."

His blood was singing all the way to the hotel. He had never been with anyone like her. Cat was her name and cat she was. A tiger cat, a man-eater, promising danger but also the possibility of great reward.

But in her hotel room he wasn't sure about the reward. He had been here before, in many rooms similar, and knew all about the building excitement of man and woman reaching toward sexual union. Lou had inferred that he was addicted to sex. But he disagreed. He never forced sex on anyone. It always came as a natural development in the mysterious chemistry where pheromones meet pheromones and mutual attraction reaches its logical result.

But Cat was something else. His being in this hotel was not a natural consequence of mutual attraction. Forced sex? The only potential victim tonight was himself. He thought again of the way she looked, standing naked and bearing the bloody head of John the Baptist. Was her kind of sexual fantasy the foreplay to a kind of death? Poor John the Baptist. Then he thought of Cindy looking at him from across the room as he rested his hand on Cat's abdomen.

Time to get out of here.

Then as he was moving toward the door it swung open, and Cat stood there in a long black coat reaching to her ankles.

"Miss me?" she asked, suddenly shrugging and the coat slid away from her shoulder, piling in a heap at her feet. She was totally naked. She leaped at him like a pit bull, slamming against his chest and wrapping her legs and arms around him. The weight caught him by surprise and he stumbled backward, losing his balance and crashing to the floor. When she sensed he was falling she quickly moved her legs out of the way and fell flat upon him.

Then she grabbed on again and bit him deep in the neck. He felt her squirming and her hands reaching toward his shirt and pants.

He couldn't believe it. She was raping him!

With one full-out heave he sent her crashing to one side, her head hitting the edge of the coffee table. She was momentarily stunned, and he quickly stumbled up.

He looked down at her and dropped the door key where it lodged between her breasts.

"Hey, Cat," he said, "I've got news for you."

Her grin still mocked him. "You're not man enough to handle it?"

"Sorry, tiger," he said, "but I've realized that life is more than a jungle."

He stayed away from the club all the next week. The girls from the Bunny Box continued to come in for workouts, but he left them on their own. Cat ignored him completely.

Then Lou phoned him at midweek and asked why he hadn't been around.

"Cat is still making them crazy every night. What I want to know is why she's not making you crazy."

"Cat and I have an understanding," Doug said.

"Some understanding. You never watch her perform anymore?"

"The best kind of understanding."

"The word around here after that first night was that Cat is too much woman for you."

"Did Cat start that rumor?" Doug asked. "But you're right Lou, Cat is too much."

Lou laughed. "I never thought I'd see Mr. Adonis cave in to a woman."

"Everyone has to retire some time, Lou."

Lou laughed, "Sure. Next month I got a crop coming in from Minneapolis. Supposed to be choice."

"Good, Lou," Doug said, and hung up.

Cindy was sitting behind the desk writing checks for some bills. She glanced briefly at him without speaking. Still cold, he thought. What a contrast be-

tween Cat and Cindy. One nice thing about Cindy—
she was real.

Later on in the morning Doug was working with
an overweight woman on a treadmill when Cindy approached him in a rush.

"Mr. Reese just phoned," she said. "He wants us to
come to his office."

They were there inside thirty minutes. Reese was
smiling as he greeted them and asked them to sit.

"I think I've got it worked out. I feel good about
it. I've taken how much you both can invest, how
much I can go for, massaged the numbers several
ways to sunshine, and I'm going to let you have
this." He handed them a folder which contained a
number of typewritten pages. "Read it over, talk it
over, discuss it with your lawyer. Any questions,
come back. But basically, this reflects what we already discussed, making it a little easier on you. If
you still think it's a good deal, then we're in business."

Doug was elated. Cindy could hardly keep from
jumping up and down. They shook hands, and agreed
to meet again in another week.

In the car Cindy's coolness had vanished. They
talked like schoolkids learning they could go home at
noon because of icy roads.

"Stop the car," Cindy suddenly said.

Surprised, he pulled over and parked. She moved
into his arms like quicksilver sliding downhill. When
he felt her lips he realized she was not like any sister.

"That was for luck, partner," she said, breathless.

Doug liked the thought of "partner," and for the
first time he opened his heart to the idea that a part-
nership with Cindy might have a deeper meaning.

But there was still one interview left, and it came a week later.

Lou Kessler was not happy.

"You're *what?*"

"I'm going to open my own place, Lou."

"You work for me."

"That's right. I'm not a partner. I just work for you, and I'm giving notice."

"You'll be competing with me."

"We don't have a contract that prohibits it."

Lou was silent a moment. "You're not stupid. Don't you know whom I represent?"

"I never wanted to know, Lou. But I can guess."

"You know we're not concerned about any written contract. What *you* should be concerned about is an unfortunate accident."

"What do you mean, Lou?"

"Things can happen, you know? And if something were to happen to you or Cindy, I would be sorry." He laughed. "I might even spring for your funeral expense I'd be so sorry."

"This doesn't sound like you, Lou. You're always so kind and considerate."

"That's why I'm telling you these things, Doug— because I care what happens to you."

Doug nodded. "Okay, Lou. I know what you can do. And even though I don't have a contract with you, you can put out a contract on me. Is that what you're saying? That you can bring in some guys from out of city as easy as you can bring girls in?"

Doug stood and moved rapidly to the door, opening it and yelling, "Hey Red Dog! Get in here!"

Doug moved back to the chair as Lou watched him curiously. Red Dog stuck his head in. "You want me, Mr. Kessler?"

"I believe that Mr. Mangrum did."

"What did you want?"

"Come on over here, Red Dog."

Red Dog moved warily to where Doug was sitting. "Take out your gun," Doug said. Red Dog looked at Lou, then slowly pulled out his gun.

"Now let me have it," Doug said, holding out his hand. Red Dog looked again at Lou, who gave a slight nod. Red Dog let Doug take the gun.

Doug held the barrel and carefully placed it to touch the side of his head. "Now take the handle," he said.

Red Dog gripped the handle and moved his head back and forth from Lou to Doug, seeking some clue as to what was happening.

"Let's make it easy on you, Lou." Doug said. "No need to cut the brake line to the master cylinder, no need to plant a bomb or order a hit-and-run or stage a mugging gone bad. If this is that big a deal just tell Red Dog to pull the trigger, and you can get rid of this small bag of potatoes here and now."

Lou looked at Red Dog. "Take off the safety."

Doug winced with the sound, but sat quietly. Lou stared at him for a long moment. Then he laughed.

"I got to hand it to you, Doug. You're bluffing. You sit there without blinking because you don't think I would have you killed right now in this office. But it's a good bluff. You're right about one thing. You *are* small potatoes. So it all boils down to—are you worth the trouble of doing something and then answering questions from the cops who'll wonder about my relationship to a former employee. But I don't like being made a sucker."

"I've been a straight employee, Lou."

"Not bad," Lou admitted. "But what about this competition problem?"

"Still small potatoes, Lou," Doug said quietly.

Lou sat quietly for another long moment. Slowly he nodded. "Take the gun away, Red Dog."

Doug began to breathe easier.

Lou stood and held out his hand. "Okay, Adonis, you're free and clear. "Only one thing," Lou said as he shook Doug's hand, "I don't want you near any of my girls, and I don't want you coming around the Bunny Box."

"You got it," Doug said.

Lou spoke his final words to Doug. "I hate to lose. And seeing you will remind me of a time when if I didn't lose, I still didn't win."

Doug started to walk away.

"One more thing. It didn't bother you, did it, when I said you had to stay away from the club and my girls?"

"I can handle it," Doug said.

"I never would have believed it, Doug Mangrum no longer interested in the best-looking women money can buy." Lou grinned. "If I were a religious man, I'd call that a miracle."

LAURA'S NEW CANE

*I first learned about Laura Armistad from the
girl I was dating. I visit a different church every
Sunday. This promotes my staying in touch—to
a degree—with the various denominations. I get
a feel for the kind of preaching taking place,
and also absorb a little of the attitude of the
congregations. I don't expect a lot of article
ideas from this practice, but you never know
when a comment or something I see might trigger an idea.*

*In any case, I decided to visit the Cumber-
land Christian Church one Sunday and was
sitting by Betty Matthews. A friend had introduced me to Betty via a blind double date, and
I had taken it from there. The fact that Betty
was a member of Cumberland Christian gave
me a reason to visit that church sooner rather
than later.*

*Cumberland Christian was situated in Cum-
berland Heights, an upscale suburb. The
grounds featured a long, winding driveway
leading to a white building with four columns*

119

and a huge steeple. An acre of concrete accommodated an army of parked cars in back.

We had arrived a little late, and were forced to sit closer to the front than I would have liked. As we moved into the pew I saw Betty nod in greeting to a girl who moved over to make room for us. She moved carefully, and I noticed she was wearing a large brace on her leg.

After the service Betty introduced me to the girl with the brace, Laura Armistad. Later when Betty and I were eating lunch in the Dallwood Cafeteria—a favorite Sunday place for the churchgoing crowd—I asked about Laura's brace.

Betty explained that she was working with Laura at the physical therapy center of East Lake Hospital. Betty was a therapist there, and Laura had been regularly coming for treatment for months, recovering from a skiing accident.

Betty said at first the doctors were afraid Laura would be paralyzed from the waist down. But she had gotten back feeling in both legs— almost a miracle.

Of course, the "miracle" idea flashed a spotlight on my attention. But I did not see Laura again until much later, when I saw an item in the newspaper. I contacted her then, and she allowed me to interview her. I had found another miracle story . . .

Laura was nervous as she sat at the table on the outside patio of Kearny's Lakeside Bar and grill, waiting for Craig to return from his phone call, and watched a speedboat in the middle of the lake dragging a teenage girl on water skis. The girl was weaving back and forth over the jarring bounce of the boat's wake. Laura looked away, not wanting to encourage a train of memories that would flash the times when she had been on water skis, watching Craig's broad back as he twisted the wheel of the runabout to send her into a wide whipping turn. She had accepted times like that as a natural birthright. All the physical activities she loved—skiing on water and in the mountains, ice skating, running—these were more than just optional opportunities that promised fun and adventure; for her they had been the natural expressions of being alive.

Until Aspen.

Craig had challenged her for a run that accelerated rapidly through a steep decline and then took off with a soaring jump lifting from a sudden rise at a cliff's edge, which then settled into a twisting run through a wooded area.

Craig had gone ahead. Laura could still vividly feel the thrill of picking up speed and then the pure surge of adrenaline as she ascended into flight. She landed safely and began the twisting and turning run through the pine trees when her skis ran over a jutted rock that had been buried under a thin layer of snow. She was airborne again, this time feeling no thrill but only the total loss of control followed by the sudden shock of blackness as her body slammed against a tree.

Laura knew the doctors were worried. She could read an encyclopedia of meaning on Craig's face as he tried to conform his words with his frozen smile. It had been her father who first told her.

She could imagine what her father had said to the doctors. Plain-speaking, bull-by-the-horns Dad. "I'll talk to her. No one else is going to tell her she might not walk again."

So Dad, who could give orders to his construction crew with the certitude of a platoon sergeant, who could correct poor performance with language that would blister the paint off the hull of an aircraft carrier, this man leaned over her hospital bed one day with moist eyes and struggled to find some words he could manage to say.

Finally, he said softly, "Laura, you remember when you were four and we went on our first hike on the Appalachian Trail?"

Laura nodded.

"Mother thought you were too young, but I persuaded her it would be all right. Remember that first day?"

Laura nodded again.

"You remember what happened about three o'clock in the afternoon?"

"I remember."

He took her hand. "You had to be carried."

Laura smiled. "I was too tired to walk anymore."

Her father sat quietly, staring at her hand. Then he looked into her eyes and spoke with a voice as soft as elderdown. "It might be time, once again, to let someone else help carry you for a while."

She stared at him. "Are you trying to say I won't be able to walk?"

"That's not certain. There's always a chance, with therapy."

"I'll walk," she said.

"I know you won't give up," he said. "After I carried you three miles that day, once we got to the next camp you got off my back and started running around as though you had never been tired in your life. So even though you need help now, think of what you might do once you're back on your feet."

She smiled. "I'll end up running around faster than ever?"

He nodded.

"I'll plan on that," she said.

The day Laura had gotten into the wheelchair for the first time had been the most traumatic. She saw it as a mechanical monster waiting to chain her to the floor. Cold and unfeeling, a symbol of her helplessness and dependence on others.

She hated it, but that changed.

It became her friend. Most normal people only visited their chairs, coming and going with little thought or awareness of where they were sitting. But her wheelchair became part of her, necessary for her movement, the faithful substitute for her legs. Furthermore, she learned every nuance of its accommodation to her body. The way it gave when she lowered her body onto the seat, the slight squeak when she made a sudden left turn, the touch of the wheels as she pushed to gain traction with the floor.

Her father had asked about a motorized chair, but she insisted on this. She wanted to push herself. At least her arms and shoulders were getting stronger.

She went back to work part time, where she and Donna Burnett were partners in a public relations agency. But she went everyday to the therapy center, performing exercises to build her strength, and waiting for some sense of feeling to return in her legs.

And then one morning it was there. A sensation of touch. The doctor pressed a pointed object against the bottom of her feet. He tapped her with what looked like a small rubber mallet to check for autonomic reflex.

He looked greatly encouraged, and before long muscles in her legs began to respond to her conscious will. She then was fitted for braces and spent a lot of time using parallel bars in willing one foot to move ahead of the other. During the long process Betty Matthews was a constant source of encouragement. And on the sidelines rooting were her parents, her partner Donna Burnett, many friends, and Craig Tyler.

Improvement continued, and the great day came when they removed the brace from Laura's left leg. Now she was using crutches, and paradoxically, she began facing her most severe times of depression and self-doubt.

The doctor explained that this often happened to people as their recovery improved. The human psyche seems to gain increased resentment of a handicap even as there seems to be cause for the greatest optimism. Perhaps it was due to the heightened impatience that wants full recovery now instead of later. Or it may trace itself to a deep belief that no matter how good the recovery, there is no way that the patient will ever be as good as he or she was before.

In any case, the doctor told her, expect those dark moods to come, and remember they will pass. The important thing was to keep on moving ahead.

Well and good, Laura thought, so while she was sitting at this table waiting for Craig to return from the phone, she could be grateful that one leg was out of the brace, and she could get around on crutches. But she still was a long way from water skis.

Craig came back to the table, smiling. "Sorry about that," he said. Craig worked at Computronics, a firm that sold, set up, and maintained computer networks. Often they dealt with large corporations already with mainframes that now wanted networks that would join them to their desktops.

"I asked Dick to phone me as soon as he got back from Denver. Looks like we may have a deal with Preston Plastics."

Laura knew that Craig was never without his cellular phone except on rare social occasions, so she imagined she should be flattered this dinner had reached that special plateau where he left his phone behind.

A man appeared for their drink order. Craig looked at Laura. She glanced at the drink menu.

"Chardonnay," she said. "The Trefethen."

"I'll have a dry Manhattan, with an extra twist of lemon," Craig said.

The man nodded and left. Craig settled back in his chair and looked out over the lake. "This is a beautiful place."

She nodded. They had been here many times. In the course of the last two years they had dined together and vacationed together and shared many activities—social as well as sport—as a "couple." This didn't mean they were officially engaged, but they were obviously heading in that direction.

Until Aspen.

Her friends thought that she and Craig were ideal for each other. They seemed totally compatible. Both young and bright, successful in business. Fun people. And her friends admired the way Craig had appeared to give her emotional support since the accident. It seemed like he didn't even notice she was on crutches, that everything between them was just as it was before the accident.

But Laura knew something was different. And in all honesty, maybe the biggest difference was in herself. She still cared for Craig. But the fact was that she was no longer free to think of herself in the same way. So many activities they had enjoyed together were no longer possible. Even the simple act of getting into and out of a car was not the same. True, Craig didn't seem to notice how careful and deliberate she was with the crutches, but lately she had come to feel that he *was* aware, that he could not help contrasting her with other women and with the way she had been.

Despite how he appeared on the surface, she felt he was having to make an increasingly conscious effort to appear unaffected by her infirmity.

The feeling bothered her, and often she told herself she was imagining his attitude, that nothing really had changed in the way they felt about each other. But they no longer seemed to talk about their future together. Their focus was on her condition, her feelings, what she was going through.

And deep down, maybe that was the way she wanted it—to focus on herself, to get better, to be as strong as she could be without worrying about her future with any man. The fact was, a lot of what she and Craig had shared was gone—all the times and activities that required two healthy, fully functioning bodies. And in facing the fact of her own altered condition, she felt she needed to adjust her expectations of what life realistically could offer. At certain times her whole relationship with Craig seemed less like a current event than an event in history.

Their drinks came, and soon they both grew pensive.

Laura's nervousness increased. Her thoughts were a jumbled mix—not knowing what he would say, not knowing what she would say, not knowing what she *wanted* to say.

She ordered a salad with ranch low-fat dressing and an entree of lemon sole. It was delicious. Craig ordered the cheese-broccoli soup followed by red snapper.

Conversation was light and rambling throughout the meal, and Craig questioned her about dessert. She shook her head. They ended with coffee, and after a sip Craig carefully set his cup down.

"I'd like to say something," he said.

Laura waited.

He looked out over the lake again, then back at her. "Did the doctor say when you might give up your crutches?"

"He thinks I'm almost ready for a cane; I'm not so sure."

He nodded, then took another sip of coffee.

"Is that what you wanted to say?" Laura asked.

He nodded, looking at his cup. "I know you'll be glad to get rid of the crutches." Then after a moment of silence he looked up at her. "I'd like to start seeing Linda."

"Linda?"

He cleared his throat. "Linda Fabertini—in the ski club."

Linda was vice president of the club, a tall, dark-haired woman who graduated last year from the University of Tennessee Law School and now worked as an assistant district attorney. She laughed a lot, and Laura liked her. She was an expert skier.

Craig was watching her carefully, and the look in his eyes made her want to smile. He didn't want to hurt her, and no matter what he said, he probably still felt a little guilty over her accident—for challenging and encouraging her to make the run. They had been a steady couple before the accident, and she might have ended up marrying him had the accident never happened. But it did. And no matter how close they had been in the past, their lives were now irrevocably different.

So be it.

She realized that unconsciously she had been expecting the breakup. And her own indecision in thinking about their future together affirmed the direction of her own thinking.

"I think that's good," she said quietly. He looked a little surprised.

"Linda's a nice girl," she added.

"You really understand?"

When she nodded he grinned and looked greatly relieved.

"I still love you," he began.

She touched his hand. "And I love you."

"But—"

She put her fingers over his lips. "You don't have to say any more. Having friends you love is one of life's greatest blessings."

When they reached her apartment building Craig started to walk her inside, but she stopped him.

He leaned forward and kissed her on the forehead. Then he straightened and started to say something, stopped, started to turn away, then said, "Look, we can still do things. Friends get together and do things."

"Sure, we can," she said.

He gave her a final smile and drove off. She watched the car until it was out of sight. She had a fleeting image of him and Linda standing on top of a mountain in Colorado, poised to begin a run, side by side.

We'll do things together, she thought, turning away and making her way up the steps. Keeping in touch by phone is doing something together.

In the hallway she heard the music coming from the apartment across from hers. Bill and Ellen Carter loved country music. Bill worked in a bank and Ellen taught school. How they ever got together had always puzzled Laura. Ellen was quiet, seldom speaking. Bill was expansive and loud.

Maybe the music. When Bill and Ellen were home something from Nashville was almost always playing on their CD player. One time in casual conversation Bill had mentioned that Sawyer Brown, Doug Stone, and Linda Davis were Ellen's favorites. He liked more of the older singers, like George Jones and Porter Waggoner.

Laura thought she recognized Sawyer Brown's "Ruby Red Shoes."

She unlocked her door and entered her apartment. A strong sense of emptiness assailed her. She made her way to the table in her dining area and sat down heavily.

It was for the best. She had wanted to break up. Her eyes blurred and she felt moistness suddenly spill down her cheek. Then she lowered her head onto her arm on the table and sobbed.

Minutes later the sobs broke up into hiccups, and she moved toward the kitchen to get a drink of water, but halfway there she realized her hiccups were gone. She changed direction and headed toward the bathroom.

She knew the breakup was the right thing. But it still hurt. She and Craig were no longer right for each other. And the thought existed that no one else would be right for her.

She went to the bathroom, washed her face, and stared at herself in the mirror. Twenty-eight, regular features with lower lip a little too full, blue eyes, heavy eyebrows, and brown, naturally wavy hair.

But from her secret room of dark imaginings came a woman's voice: *A beautiful face, my dear, but isn't it too bad about her leg?* And then another voice, a male voice: *Good figure. She'd be a knockout without the crutches.*

Laura moved to her favorite chair and tried to watch TV. Cop shows, reality shows, pseudo-news shows that hyped tawdry tales into sensational exposés, mindless sitcoms that used recorded laugh tracks to sweeten the audience response. Not worth watching. None of the jewel shows were in tonight's morass. She clicked off the remote.

Empty screen, empty life.

She wanted something cold to drink. Rising, she started toward the kitchen. Every move from room to room becomes a voyage, she thought, of days and days. Wagons westward. If the pioneers could make it to Oregon on the Oregon Trail, she could make it to the refrigerator.

The ice maker wasn't working. No ice. She slammed the door. She would not be defeated by an ice maker.

Slowly she made her way out her door and across the hallway and knocked on the Carters' door. The door opened to disclose Ellen holding what looked like a glass of orange juice.

"Laura," she exclaimed, "the music too loud for you?"

Laura shook her head. "I wonder if I could borrow some ice?"

"Of course, come in."

Laura saw Bill in a chair near the couch, also holding a glass of the orange drink. Another man was on the couch. Laura quickly catalogued him as a thirtysomething, under six feet, wearing dark-framed glasses, a brown sport jacket, and white turtleneck shirt—and looking intellectual. Ellen introduced him as Michael Donnely, an English teacher at the high school where she taught.

"Sit down," Ellen invited. Laura said she had to go, but Ellen insisted.

"Let me get you a drink."

"That orange juice does look good," Laura said, sitting.

Ellen smiled. "These are Bulldogs. You'll like it."

Laura noticed that Michael was looking at her brace.

"A skiing accident," she said.

"I do a little skiing," he said.

"Do you know about the ski club?" she asked.

"No."

"It's very active. One major trip a year and three more on a minor scale."

"Where did you get hurt?" he asked.

"Aspen."

"Laura is making a good recovery," Ellen said, handing Laura her drink and then turning down the music. "Probably won't be long until she's using a cane."

Laura smiled and sipped the drink. "This is good," she said.

"A Bulldog is easy to make," Ellen said. "Orange

juice in a tall glass, two jiggers of gin, and fill up with ginger ale."

"I prefer a Dog's Nose," Bill grinned. "Two jiggers of gin in a tall glass filled up with cold beer."

"Who comes up with those names?" Laura wondered.

"Probably some alcoholic veterinarian," Michael said.

The conversation flowed and Laura discovered that Michael had a good sense of humor and was working on a novel about guilt in a New England town. "Of course," he grinned, "if that doesn't sell I've got an idea for one about love among the magnolias—set in a southern town."

"Like this town?" Laura asked.

"Could be," he said, and that ended his talk about book ideas. He said he never talked out his ideas in public before writing them. Talk dissipated creativity, he said.

Laura said that might be true with novels, but talking enhanced creativity in her line of work. Brainstorming generated ideas in the spark of give and take among different individuals.

Sometime later in the evening as she finished her second Bulldog, Laura realized it was getting late. She was also surprised that she had had a good time. So much for romantic entanglements. Craig who?

She grinned wryly, and then was conscious of how slowly she stood up. Michael didn't offer to help her stand. She liked Michael.

"Just a minute," Ellen said. "I just thought of something." She disappeared into her bedroom, and came out a moment later with a cane.

This was a cane unlike any Laura had seen. A homemade cane, obviously. Some kind of dark wood with light blotches that looked like where branches had been cut off. The wood had been shaped with a knife, then sanded, varnished, and shellacked until it glistened like a thin coating of ice. A rubber stopper was on the bottom for traction.

"This was my grandfather's." Ellen said. "The only keepsake I have from him. He used it for more than ten years when I was growing up. He lived with us until he was eighty-seven. Died of intestinal cancer. Why don't you borrow it and maybe practice with it when you're able?"

Ellen smiled. "It's not very pretty, so you may never want to use it in public, but my granddad made it and I would be happy if you could get some use out of it."

"It's a beautiful cane," Laura said, taking it and imagining the miles and the years of service it must have had. She hoped her own need for it would be much more short term.

The next morning Laura lay in bed and didn't want to get up. She knew it was getting late, and if she didn't get into the office Donna would be calling her. When she sat up on the bed the first thing she saw was the wooden cane she had propped against her dressing table when she fell into bed last night.

She immediately had fallen to sleep, but her sleep was fitful. Images flashed by of her childhood, her first attempt at riding a bike, her first time on ice skates. Each time she fell. But her worst dream was when she was in a spelling bee in the third grade. She and her rival Carolyn Weathers were the only two left. And Laura had been asked to spell "beautiful." Laura had called out an "e" to follow the "t." Carolyn won. And out on the playground at recess Carolyn had made a face at her and said, "You lost.

I'm better than you. Yah, yah," and then ran toward
the jungle gym with two other girls chasing after her.

Now the cane seemed to be saying to her, "You
lost."

Laura reached for her brace, and fixed it around
her leg. She pulled her crutches up from the floor and
determinedly got to her feet. The cane wasn't talking
to her. Her silly dreams were talking, and they were
mute in daylight.

She picked up the cane. This would be her symbol
of victory, not defeat. "You lost," Carolyn had said.
Laura hated to lose. But as she made her way to the
bathroom, Laura knew how easy it was to be depressed.

Burnett-Armistad had a suite on the second floor
of a two-story building on Twenty-fourth Street. The
hallway was carpeted with dark blue pile that blended
with the light gray walls. Inside the suite Carol—the
receptionist—was on the phone, but she motioned for
Laura to stop. She covered the phone and spoke
softly to Laura. "Donna has someone in her office.
She wants you to go right in."

Donna was a heavy-set woman of thirty-five, and
she looked relieved to see Laura.

"Laura, this is Mr. Bob Milburn. Bob—Laura
Armistad."

After Laura was seated, Donna went on. "Laura, I
met Bob at last night's meeting of the state film commission. He has a project where we might contribute.
Bob, would you like to fill Laura in?"

He smiled. "Why, sure." He spoke with a southern
accent. "I'm one of the investors in a limited partner-
ship that was formed to produce an independent film.
Not one of those thirty-million-dollar Hollywood deals.
Shot the whole thing in this state. Used country music

stars out of Nashville. Brought in New York actors to fill the parts requiring real acting. Picked up a director out of Hollywood. Mainly local guys on the crew. Almost all the scenes were shot on location. Where we're spending extra money to be sure everything looks grade A professional is on our music—we have an original score and we're getting it recorded in London, where it can be done cheaper than anywhere in this country. And then we're post-dubbing all the dialogue tracks in New York. Sound isn't too good on location. Nothing makes a film look as amateurish as poor sound quality."

Laura nodded through all this, learning more than she really wanted to know. Finally, he grinned.

"Guess you can tell I'm excited. Isn't everyday a guy who owns an auto parts place in a small town like Jackson gets to be a movie producer. But Jeff Pearson—he had the idea. He was a drama major in Western Kentucky, and he wants to write. He came up with this screenplay. And the idea was—what kind of film can be produced on a relatively low budget and still have enough box office appeal that theaters will want to book it and people will want to see it?"

He looked at Laura expectantly. She said nothing, so he continued. "Did you know that one-fifth of all records sold today is country? Rock and roll is still the most popular, but country has moved up to twenty percent of the market. The hottest male performer in music is not a rock and roller—but Garth Brooks. So we made a movie with lots of country music, and got some big names to appear, but still and all—we center on a story with universal appeal—a love story."

Again he stopped. Laura thought this wasn't the

most original idea she had ever heard, and she knew
something of other independent films about country
music that had bombed.

"Well," he said, "we've got it in the can and the
rough cuts look fine, and a date for recording the
score is set for next month."

"Who's distributing the film?" Laura asked.

"Well, we have no track record of past success, so
we couldn't get a pre-production deal. When we get
it all together we'll shop it around in Hollywood.
Distributors are always glad to look at your product,
and we're confident enough in it we think if we don't
get a major distributor, we can release it indepen-
dently."

He laughed. "It's not that we've got to make a for-
tune to break even. Those Hollywood types would
faint if they knew how little we are spending. They
need fifty million box office to break even on a typical film. We can break even on one-tenth that
amount."

"How can we help you?" Laura asked.

"The state film commission helped us a lot—in lo-
cating crew, making contact with the agents of the
country artists, in some cases going straight to the
artist. So we want to hold a big premiere here, and
we would like a PR outfit to work with us in planning the whole shebang."

Laura leaned back in her chair. This guy had the
manner of a country cousin ripe for plucking by big
city operators. But somehow she thought that impression was false. For one thing the substance of what
he said seemed to display a good deal of solid knowledge about the film business. She had heard horror
stories of how a major distributor could rip off an independent producer in accounting for the theater re-

ceipts. But a good film and a good lawyer could go a long way toward firming up an honest deal. In any case, this project would be one of the more interesting ones they would have had all year.

They did some more talking about fees and costs, and the meeting ended up with a handshake, and the understanding that Burnett-Armistad would develop a contract that he could share with his partners for final approval.

During the next three weeks Laura rode an elevator of constant ups and downs. Mood shifts took her to ground floor where depression swirled like North Sea fog moving in on the Scottish coast, and then she was taken up to a floor above the fog where she could lose herself in work. Michael Donnelly called her twice during that time to ask her out for dinner, but she refused him. She did not want to see anyone.

The thought of Craig was no problem. But she had no confidence that she would be able to sustain her emotions on an even keel for the block of time required for a date.

The leg and the brace and the crutches were always with her. Only in work could she lose awareness of her infirmity. And then at the therapy center she could handle it in another way—not in losing awareness but in facing it head on and defiantly struggling against it with the machines and the parallel bars.

During the third week Betty Matthews spotted something while Laura worked on the parallel bars. She wanted Laura to try and take two steps without support. Laura tried it, and fell into Betty's arms.

"Your leg is stronger," Betty exclaimed. "Can you feel it?"

"I would have fallen if you hadn't caught me."

"But you took one step. You're stronger. Before long maybe you'll be on a cane."

During the following two weeks Laura worked harder than ever with the machines and the parallel bars. She was able to take a few steps walking between the bars. Then they tried her with a cane, and she took tentative steps.

Two more weeks, and now Laura felt confident enough to divorce the crutches and go steady with the cane.

Plans were firming up for the premiere of the film, which was now titled *Country Cool*. Laura felt they might have had a better chance for a hit if they had gotten Paul Newman in it and called it *Country Cool Hand Luke*. But she hoped for the best. She liked Bob Milburn and some of his infectious excitement had invaded her more temperate disposition.

Michael Donnely had called her twice more, and now she was feeling a little guilty. But she was really busy now. The big event had shaped up as the film showing, with spotlighted arrivals of city fathers and music celebrities in limousines, sidewalk interviews by a top country deejay, and afterward a formal dinner party for selected guests at the Rich Meade Country Club.

Laura didn't have time to think about Michael, but then two weeks ahead of the premiere Bob Milburn invited her to attend with him. She thanked him profusely but lied and said she already had a date. She would have enjoyed going with Bob, but between him and Michael, Laura had no doubt which one should receive her first consideration.

Of course, if Michael couldn't go, she'd have to figure out another story for Bob.

She needn't have worried. Michael was delighted with the invitation, and slightly stunned after being turned down several times for a date.

Laura selected an ankle-length red satin gown that bared one shoulder and gave her a chance to show off some new pearl earrings she found at Abernathy-Payne. As she studied herself in the full-length mirror she had to admit that she looked about as good as she ever had. But that metal cane was as jarring as chocolate syrup resting on a bed of lettuce.

Okay. She still needed a cane. She went to the closet and pulled out the wooden cane that Ellen Carter had loaned her. Maybe it looked funny, but it wasn't as cold or clinical as the metal cane. And anyway, the film was country all the way, and this cane would feel right at home in the hand of any farmer walking down any dusty country road.

Michael came by for her in his two-year-old Camry. Opening the door, she stood before him holding a matching red clutch purse covered with sequins that teased the light, and in the other hand a homemade wooden cane.

He had trouble speaking, but finally got out, "You're beautiful." And for the first time she thought her mood elevator might not be taking her down so far anymore. She'd get off at the top floor and try to stay there. And even though she liked this cane, she had the feeling she wouldn't be using it very long.

She told him where to park, about half a block away from the front of the theater, in a side lot beside a vacant department store. They walked slowly on the sidewalk toward the crowd and commotion of cars arriving, celebrities giving street interviews, and photographers firing off their cameras.

Just as they were nearing the edge of the crowd, a

man who was backing up suddenly turned and bumped head-on into Michael, who stumbled backward. The man began apologizing, and at that moment another man grabbed at Laura's purse. She held on and yelled. Michael turned toward her and the man gave another jerk, tearing the purse away. Then he turned to run.

At that moment without thinking Laura had both hands gripping the cane and swung it around in a low arc. The crook of the handle circled one ankle and as the man tried to step forward he fell flat on his face. A photographer's flash went off and then Michael knelt on the man's back, holding the man's wrist. One of the policemen immediately appeared and took custody.

The rest of the evening went by without incident, and afterward the buzz was that *Country Cool* was one of the best country music films yet. Maybe *the* best.

The next day Laura's picture appeared in the paper. She was holding a wooden cane with the crook near her face. And a man was being handcuffed by an officer. The brief article described the quick thinking of Laura Armistad in using such a unique method of catching a mugger.

That morning a man was standing at a street corner waiting for a city bus when he noticed a nearby woman reading the paper.

"What'd you think about that woman with the cane?" the man asked.

The woman looked up at him. "I think here's a woman who has it all together."

BILL'S BIKE

Ever since I owned a Raleigh Rampar when I was a kid I've been in love with bikes. When I was thirteen my dad bought me a Schwinn Varsity ten-speed that saw me through high school. When I got out of college, though, my grown-up activities such as work and the other sundry pressures of making it as an adult distracted me from my early loyalty to the world of two-wheelers. But I never forgot the sense of freedom and the thrill of self-propelled speed that highlighted the time of my youth.

After I got settled in my new job I became curious about the T-Bikers Club I saw mentioned in the paper. I made contact with the club's secretary, and attended the next monthly meeting that was held at Romeer's Restaurant. There I met the club president, Bill Mercer, who owned the Peddlers Open Air and Bike Emporium. I talked to him after the meeting and found him very personable. About thirty-seven, slightly shorter than my six feet three height, with auburn hair and skin that looked like it belonged to a road-weary veteran of the bike wars. The

*sun and the wind had left evidence of their close
acquaintanceship. I told him I might be interested in a new bike, and he invited me to visit
Peddlers.*

*I settled on a Raleigh, drawn that way by the
memory of my first bike. But this Raleigh Touring was a different breed from the Rampar. My
old bike had three speeds, the Touring fourteen
speeds, able to carry me on a 23½-inch frame
weighing twenty-eight pounds at a speed guaranteed to bring the rosy flush of youth to any
pallid adult face.*

*Club members planned excursions that
ranged from one-day runs to trips that might
take a week. I made new friends in the club, and
became especially close to Bill, but early on
never felt that he might be a possible miracle
story. I was wrong . . .*

Bill had worked late at the shop getting Ted
Dorsey's bike ready for a track race in St. Louis. Ted
was one of the better racers in the state, specializing
in track. He had competed on some of the better
tracks in the U.S., including ones in Shakopee, Min-
nesota, Milwaukee, Encino, and Northbrook, Illinois.
Unlike road bikes, many manufacturers do not sell a
completely equipped track bike since cyclists are
highly subjective in choosing their components.

So Ted had ordered a Nishiki frame which was
chrome molybdenum double-butted tubing. To it Bill
was adding a Campagnolo crankset, sprocket, hubs,
and pedals; Windsor saddle, tires, and rims; and Galli
brakes. Total weight would be eighteen pounds.

A high-pitched voice caught Bill's attention. Kathy

was standing at the door to the office. "I've finished stuffing those flyers into the envelopes, Mr. Mercer."

"I told you to call me Bill, Kathy."

She grinned and flipped her head so that her pale blond hair momentarily waved like a banner in a strong wind. Then came a modest downward glance of her eyes, which then rebounded from the floor straight into his own eyes. He felt the impact.

He was forty-nine, but that didn't keep him from recognizing that Kathy had the power to make him forget all about age. Like the old radio Shadow, she had the power to "cloud men's minds."

Bill hadn't wanted to hire her. She was built better than any bike in the place, and he wasn't sure he could get his customers to look at bike accessories after they saw her accessories.

"Don't hold her looks against her," Mike had told him. Mike Holden ran the pet shop across the street. "She's a good worker, but my wife would go crazy if I kept her around. And I've got to admit I'd be tempted to try something." He laughed. "An old geezer like you shouldn't have any trouble."

"I'm married, too," Bill said.

"Yeah," Mike laughed, "like Holly would ever be worried. You're married to the most beautiful woman in the city, next to my wife, of course. I still can't believe you knew Holly in college. She looks fifteen years younger."

Bill couldn't get angry, because Mike was telling the truth. Holly *was* beautiful, and she didn't look much over thirty. Besides, Mike recently had bought a Windsor Professional from him, so he could safely say anything.

"I still don't know—" Bill said.

"Give her a chance. I told her I'd speak to you.

She likes you." Mike grinned. "She's commented how good looking you are."

Bill thought a moment. He had interviewed three women in the past week to take Mrs. Porter's place. Hadn't liked any of them.

"Okay. Have her come over for an interview."

She had started working for him yesterday, and so far he liked her enthusiasm about the work. Like tonight, she volunteered to stay late and help him get out a publicity mailing for the forthcoming Hillcrest Scramble road race that was co-sponsored by Peddlers and the T-Biker Club.

"No problem," she said. "I was waiting around for Daryl to finish, anyway."

She talked nonstop while they were stuffing envelopes.

"I never realized that you sold so many different things besides bikes."

"Most bikers are interested in broader aspects of the outdoor life. Camping gear and exercise equipment were a natural extension for us." They finished the last of the envelopes.

She smiled. "I'm surprised about the exercise equipment. I thought bikes would be enough exercise for anyone."

He laughed. "Come on over here," he motioned to follow him as he walked to a stationary exercycle. "Try to pedal," he said, twisting a knob.

She got on and made an effort. "This is hard."

He nodded. "You can rig the resistance to develop leg strength in a different way from bikes. Biking builds strength for endurance. This equipment builds raw strength, which can come in handy when pulling up a hill, like I'll be doing in the Hillcrest Scramble."

"You'll be in the race?"

He nodded. "I've entered every Scramble since the first one eleven years ago. It's a tough one—ten miles over the steep hills in Hillcrest Park."

"You look like you're in good shape," she said.

He grinned. "Not good enough. I'll be spending time on this exercycle every day until two days before the race."

At that moment Daryl stuck his head in the doorway leading to the repair room. "I've finished Mr. Ordwell's bike."

"Thanks, Daryl," Bill said. "Ordwell would have shot me if we didn't fix his bike so he could take it when he leaves town tomorrow."

Daryl approached them and looked at Kathy. "You about ready to leave?"

She nodded. Bill grinned to himself. Daryl was a fast worker. Then Kathy looked at Bill. "We're going to Dave's Diner. Have you ever been there?"

"No."

"It's a great place to relax and have a beer or something," she said. "Would you like to come with us?"

Daryl looked startled. "Yeah, Bill, why don't you come with us." His heart wasn't in it.

Bill shook his head. "I need to work out a little and then get home. Thanks anyway."

When Daryl and Kathy reached the door she stopped and turned back. "Good night, Bill. See you tomorrow."

"Good night," he said, watching them walk out of sight past the window. That's that I need, he thought, to go somewhere and drink some beer with a girl like Kathy. He got a pair of shorts he kept in his desk drawer, turned the resistance high on the exercycle, and began pumping like crazy.

When Bill pulled into the driveway he saw the house was dark. Holly was still out. Surprise, surprise.

The garage door opened to his remote, and he pulled inside. Slamming the car door behind him, he stared at his workbench and the half-finished chair he was building for his wife's dressing table. He loved woodworking, and wanted to get into some serious pieces, like a new dining table.

He shrugged off the thought. Forget the table. His wife wasn't home enough for them ever to use it, anyway.

He walked through the kitchen to the den, turning lights on. He ought to get a dog, something alive that would welcome him when he came home. A four-legged life form that would cut through the empty stillness that felt like a tomb. He went to the CD player and picked up an Andy Williams album that featured his early hits.

When he turned up the volume he was ready for the burst when the sound hit. He was always surprised to hear the early Andy when he was a teen idol, singing with high energy and bouncy beat and high volume. He was a real bubblebath of verve and enthusiasm back then, long before he became the unflappable smooth crooner of "Moon River."

Bill went to the refrigerator and took out a bottle of Coors and went back to the den and sank into his recliner. His wife was busy now. And always would be in her new job.

He had met Holly at college when he almost ran over her while he was making a dash on his bike from one class to another in a building across the galaxy. She was with two other girls and he was looking in another direction (at another girl) when they stepped into his path. He swerved and skidded on loose rocks, hitting the ground. The other two girls were laughing, but only Holly expressed concern for his welfare.

As they got to know each other they realized they were very different from one another, but somehow that didn't seem to matter. Both were business majors, but that's where the similarity stopped. Bill told her how one day he wanted to take over his father's bike shop. He had grown up with bikes, visiting his father's shop often and watching mechanics work. Then he would slip into the showroom and watch the people when they came in and asked his father questions about the new bikes.

He loved to ride bikes, disdaining the motorized two-wheelers as he got older, and looked forward to making a living out of a profession that for him would be as much fun as work.

Bill's sense of boyish enthusiasm appealed to Holly, who was far more serious in outlook. She wanted to work in a hospital—not as a doctor or nurse—but in administration. Her father was a doctor, and he had encouraged her to think of medicine. But she had watched her mother slowly die of cervical cancer. She had seen her mother day after day as a patient, and knew that she did not want to deal directly with other people who were patients, who might—like her mother—be facing a slow, lingering, and painful process of dying.

But she did want to feel that she was participating in some way in her father's profession, helping people receive medical treatment and recover good health. She felt comfortable in the hospital environment.

So she and Bill helped bring out dormant aspects

of each other's personality. She made him more sensitive to serious matters, and he helped her better understand that life needed an element of fun and adventure. Friends thought they complemented each other.

After graduating they married and Bill started working at his father's bike establishment. With time he altered the flavor of the store to more of an outdoor, camping motif, rather than strictly selling and servicing bicycles. But the die-hard bikers, the serious ones either in racing or touring, knew they could still get the exclusive kind of attention and knowledge at Peddlers that they demanded at their level of skill and experience.

Bill chugged down a little more of his Coors. It was ironic, he thought. During the early years of their marriage he had been the one who kept the late hours, who was away from home much of the time. For one thing the T-Biker Club took a lot of time. It was a fun club to join, but he also felt his active participation would benefit him professionally. He was soon in the middle of their planning activities—the tours, the races, the bike-ins for outdoor camping.

And then there was the planning for new lines of equipment at the store as he expanded into broader outdoor pursuits. Also during this time his father had retired, forcing Bill to expend even more time on the business. And always there was the specialized demand for fitting components onto custom bikes. Customers paid him well for this kind of attention. Many a rising thirtysomething executive still felt the call to the open road, and was willing to pay for the best equipment. And the racers were the most demanding of all, insisting on the lightest equipment made. In the world of biking, less costs more.

When Holly had started at Northside Hospital her job was strictly eight to five. Starting at a relatively low level in the office of the Rehabilitation Center, she was soon transferred to the Counseling Center Department. She proved good with records and administration, and was later promoted to administrative assistant in the Corporate Health Services Department. Always ambitious, taking her work seriously, and making a good impression in her personal relationships, her next promotion took her to the Communications Department.

This turned out to be a strategic move for her, since Roger Hollawell, the hospital president, took a personal interest in this department. He utilized celebrity types to endorse the hospital on TV, and was highly conscious of all the PR and promotional functions that would spotlight the hospital to the general public. Holly was active in developing a number of these events, and more than once managed to place the president's picture in the newspaper as part of followup publicity. This was not unnoticed by the president.

During this time while Holly was in communications, Bill first began to be concerned about how much time she was having to spend at the hospital. But the real surge of all-hours activity came when she received her latest promotion.

The president, impressed with Holly's efficiency and attitude, called her into his office, and outlined a job that would involve her in learning about almost every phase of the hospital's operation. He wanted her to be his executive assistant. He explained he wasn't able to appear at all the meetings that he would like—the hospital had too many departments and centers for the kind of close contact he would like, including the Drug and Alcohol Recovery Center, the Psychiatric Center, the Rehabilitation Center, and the Sports Medicine Center, among others. He wanted to be a hands-on administrator, and he felt the best he could do would be to find someone he trusted to serve as the representative and liaison for his office in many of the meetings where his presence would be helpful but where he couldn't possibly be in person. This person could represent his office and report back to him on any pressing matters or complaints.

Naturally, he said, this person would receive an appropriate salary, and be called on to devote a great deal of time to the hospital. He also talked a little about the vice president and how he would function in relation to the executive assistant. Holly was glad to accept the new position. She talked it over with Bill, who tried to hide his mixed emotions. If he already was bothered by her spending so much time at the hospital, what would it be like with the new job? At the same time he knew how serious she was about her career. Her drive and ambition were part of her basic nature. He did not want to interfere with that, or stand in her way. So he did not voice objections, except to ask one question:

"Why doesn't he use his vice president as his liaison?"

"He said the vice president's main function was to concentrate on funding for capital needs."

Bill nodded, but inside he wondered when he and Holly would be able to get on their bikes and take off for a weekend camping trip to Lake Meriwether again.

He was putting down his empty bottle of Coors when lights from the driveway flashed across the window, breaking his reverie. He hurried to the door, opening it as Holly came in with a smile. She was carrying a bag of groceries. Giving him a quick kiss, she moved to the counter and set down the bag.

"I picked up some deli things from Hill's," she said. "Salad and sliced turkey sound all right?"

"Sure thing," he said, taking her in his arms and giving her a warmer greeting.

"I have to get back by seven-thirty. Dr. McNabb is meeting with his doctors in Reconstructive Surgery to talk about some new equipment."

"How do the department heads feel about your coming to their meetings?"

"They're not threatened. They know I'm a sounding board more than anything else. And since the president can't be everywhere, they know a human face might help them more than a letter, a written report, or E-mail. So I think most of them are glad to see me."

He smiled. "I'm glad to see you, too."

She came into his arms again. "It seems like you and I don't see much of each other these days," she said.

"And nights," he added.

Holly busied herself at the counter, placing the food on plates. She poured herself a glass of mineral water and hurriedly sat down at the table.

"Want some?"

"No, thanks." He began to eat slowly.

"How was your day?" she asked.

"Pretty good. Sold five bikes. Quite a bit of camping stuff. Got Ordwell's bike ready for him. Got the new mailing for the race ready to go out. A number of entries came back today from last week's mailing."

"You're still planning to race?" she asked.

"Wouldn't miss it."

"After your spill last month I hoped you'd reconsider."

"My leg's okay."

"At least do the shorter run."

He shook his head. "I wouldn't feel right not doing the ten."

"Level ground is one thing, but those hills at your age—"

" 'My age'?" he interrupted.

"Yes," she nodded. "Your age. You weren't even forty when you ran in your first Scramble."

"I'm in pretty good shape."

"I know, but you're still pushing fifty, just like I am."

He didn't feel near fifty, just as she didn't look near fifty. He often wondered how it would have been if they had been able to have children. The third year when they had tried for pregnancy had been frightening. Holly bled heavily and suffered severe lower back pain. Cancer was foremost in their minds when she went to the doctor. The diagnosis was endometriosis, and she was treated with danazol. But the doctor warned them that thirty to forty percent of women with endometriosis were infertile. They discovered they fell within the unlucky percentage.

But if they had had children, how would they have been feeling now? Would the extra wear and tear have taken a physical toll, making them feel old as they left their forties? They never would know, but he knew how he felt, and he sure didn't feel old now.

Holly took another bite of her sliced turkey sandwich. "Oh," she said, "how is the new girl working out?"

"After one day—fine," he said.

"Did you ever find out why she quit the pet shop?"

He hesitated. "Not really, but the timing for me was good."

He stared at her for a moment. "I'll tell you what," he said. "I'll drop down to the 4.8-mile race if you enter."

She looked at him as though he was crazy. "You're kidding!"

He shook his head. "You enter the Scramble and I'll take the easy course." Actually, the 4.8 course was not that easy, but it was far less demanding than the ten-mile course.

"I'm not in shape," she said.

"You could handle the 1.8-mile run. Be good for you. We haven't done anything like this together for a long time. How about it?"

She stared at him. "I know we don't seem to do much anymore, but not the race. I think I'll be busy that weekend working on a report for the hospital trustees who'll be meeting the following Tuesday."

He slowly nodded. She reached out and put her hand on his arm. "I'm sorry, Bill. We'll do something before long."

"When?" he asked.

"This is a busy time right now."

"You'll always be busy as long as you have that job." His voice carried an intensity that made her stop talking.

"You knew how it would be," she said.

"That doesn't mean I like it."

Her voice hardened. "We talked about this. You agreed—"

He nodded. "You're right, I agreed. You're right."

She stared at him. He continued. "This house is empty without you. My life is empty without you."

She slowly stood up. "I need to get back," she said. "We'll talk some more."

He sat without moving as she left the house. The headlights flashing across the window were like a final wave good-bye.

The next day Bill spent a lot of his time in the effort of trying not to look at Kathy. She wore a yellow miniskirted dress with yellow hose and black flats—looking very young.

He and Holly had not done any more talking. She got back too late last night and this morning she told him not to plan on her for dinner and she wouldn't be home until late again tonight.

Kathy's attitude toward him all day was cool and correct. His musings last night about her had been fun in fantasyland. If he were still single and fifteen years younger . . . He caught himself staring at Kathy several times during the afternoon, and as the day wore he grew more edgy. Another lonely house tonight.

At closing time he watched to see if Daryl and Kathy would get together. The men from the back all left. His last two sales clerks left, along with his two office workers. Kathy seemed to linger in the office, and then Daryl approached her.

"Ready?" he asked. She nodded.

"Good night, Bill," she said.

"Good night, Kathy, Daryl," Bill said.

They started to walk away and Bill cleared his throat. "You two going to Dave's Diner?"

Kathy turned and nodded. "Yes."

"Do you mind if I join you?"

"Of course not," Kathy said. Daryl said nothing. In the parking lot Bill started to move away from them.

"I'll meet you there," he said.

"Why don't I go in your car," Kathy said, leaving Daryl looking less than thrilled.

Bill felt his heart beating faster as he held the door open for her. When he got in he noticed she had moved toward the center. As he started the car and directed it through the traffic, he was keenly aware of her hand resting on the seat near his leg.

He grimaced, feeling like he was back in high school again.

Dave's Diner was reputed to produce the best cheeseburgers in town. But its major role was to serve as a smoke-filled oasis where the after-work crowd could relax, dance, or watch one of two large video screens with the sound turned off. Beer was all but mandatory.

Bill hated smoke. He could almost feel the little carcinogens crawling down his nasal passages in a mad rush to reach his lungs. An old-time jukebox was in one corner playing old-time music that he had danced to during the Friday night dances in the school gym after the basketball game. He had always liked the slow dances. No other feeling like it. With the right girl it was pure magic.

Then while he looked at Kathy, who was laughing at something Daryl said, Artie Shaw's "Dancing in the Dark" began, a song from a generation even earlier than his. But he liked the number—talk about the ideal slow dance tune. Without thinking, he touched Kathy's arm.

"Would you like to dance?"

Her eyes widened, but she nodded yes with a smile.

As they moved to the floor Bill cringed inside. He realized no one else was dancing. He felt like he was moving in the spotlight of the world with the total population of creation staring at him.

She moved easily into his arms and without any prompting from him pressed closely against him. A feeling came over him that he hadn't experienced in a very long time. A warm, glowing feeling that makes the present moment of sharing closeness with someone a magic carpet ride over a land of pure enchantment. For a few moments he lost the awareness of where he was, letting himself float to every sliding gradation of the music, and then he smelled the cigarette smoke, saw the video screens with their silent moving images, and knew he was holding the wrong woman.

When the dance ended he stepped back from Kathy and smiled, noticing how wide and blue her eyes seemed. As he led her back to the table he had a good idea of a certain story that would pass around among the guys in the service department next day.

The rest of his time in Dave's Diner was a careful charade of polite talk covering up his anxiety to leave.

"I need to get home," he said finally. "Thanks for letting me barge in on you guys. I enjoyed it. See you tomorrow."

Kathy's eyes seemed to hold a question, but he quickly smiled and walked away.

In the car driving home, he pounded the steering wheel. Stupid, stupid, stupid. Not that he had done anything horribly wrong, but Daryl would be talking, and Bill didn't like the idea of whispers behind his back.

But what had he really done? Danced one dance

with an attractive young woman. No—make that a *beautiful, very young* woman who was young enough to be his daughter.

It was stupid. No other word for it. But what had he really done?

Okay, he obviously enjoyed it. The expression on his face, his entire attitude, the way he acted—all must have shouted to anyone with half an interest, and certainly to Daryl that here was a guy momentarily caught up on the romantic haze of a mid-life crisis.

And this guy was married to a woman like Holly! He shook his head. He and Holly had to do some more talking. If his homelife were contributing to the wayward thoughts of a man who was missing his wife, some changes needed to be made.

Otherwise, he thought, he'd have to spend enough hours pumping the pedals on that exercycle so that when he staggered home an exhausted husk of a man he would have nothing on his mind except the need for immediate sleep.

When he arrived home he was surprised to see lights on in the house.

"I called your office to tell you I changed my plans and would be home tonight," she said.

"I'm sorry," he said. "I stopped off at Dave's Diner for a beer. Daryl goes there quite a bit."

"You were with Daryl?"

He nodded. "And Kathy was there."

"Did you eat there?" she asked.

"I wasn't hungry."

"Let's go get a cheeseburger," she said.

He looked hesitant.

"Come on."

"I'm still not hungry."

She grabbed his arm. "Drink coffee. We can talk."

"Daryl and Kathy may still be there."

"We don't have to sit with them, particularly since you just left them. Come on."

He let himself be dragged away.

The place was more crowded than ever. Daryl and Kathy were still there. Bill led Holly to their table. Daryl was holding a can of beer. Kathy kept her eyes solidly glued to Bill.

"Hi, again," Bill said. "We're going to be sitting at that table over there, but I wanted Holly to meet Kathy."

He introduced them, and it seemed to him both were observing details about each other that he could not even guess at.

"It's nice to meet you, Mrs. Mercer."

"Holly, please," Holly smiled. "I hope you'll enjoy working at Peddlers."

"I like it already," Kathy said.

Walking away, Holly whispered, "What she likes is you."

"Why do you say that?" Bill whispered back as they sat at the table.

"I just know."

Bill would have laughed at her if he hadn't been feeling guilty about his earlier feelings. He was glad the waiter came. Holly ordered a cheeseburger with everything except mayo, mustard added, and French fries. Bill ordered coffee. When the waiter left, Tommy Dorsey came on with "Night and Day." Another favorite in the classic slow dance category.

Bill looked at Holly and she had the same idea. Without speaking she held out her hand and they moved to the dance floor. Again he was alone on the floor with a dance partner. He wondered if anyone near would remember his earlier visit. He could imagine the dialogue at their table.

"Isn't it nice the way that guy danced with his daughter and then went home and got his wife?"

Cole Porter's song weaved its usual spell, and Bill felt his arm exerting ever-tighter pressure on Holly's back. Once, over Holly's shoulder, he spotted Kathy looking intently at them with a quizzical expression.

Sorry, kid, he thought—no contest.

At home later he and Holly had a heart-to-heart talk. Bill was apologetic about the way he talked last night. She stopped him.

"I was upset at first," she admitted, "but then today as I thought about it I realized it was kind of silly to be upset when your husband tells you he misses you and wants to spend more time with you."

"Look," Bill said, "I know how important your work is to you. And I'm proud of what you've achieved. I can handle it."

"Not alone you can't," she said. "We can handle it together."

He leaned forward and kissed her, which led to something else, which in turn led to something else, which then led to the bedroom, and something else . . .

Somehow the next morning when he woke, everything seemed a lot better. And continued so in the following days and weeks. The hospital demands stayed the same. She was still gone a lot, but he felt like he was reliving the first year of his marriage. Her absence simply generated a boiler of steam that kept building in intensity until she got home and faced the inevitable results. Bill was glad she was a good engineer who knew how to relieve the pressure.

* * *

The layout of the race course for the Hillcrest Scramble allowed bikers at all levels to participate. The advanced riders took on the ten-mile course over numerous hills of steep grade. The intermediate riders could choose the 4.8 miles that covered easier terrain. The 1.8-mile run was for beginners and those not in good shape.

The starting times were staggered with the advanced bikers beginning first, way ahead of the last group. The early bikers would not even see most of those who started later. But at the tail end of the course, all trails intersected so that a ten-mile biker might catch up and pass a 1.8 biker.

Bill was sorry that Holly had not changed her mind about entering the 1.8-mile run. He felt great. His work on the exercycle paid off. He also felt great about Kathy at work. No more tension between them, no more calculating glances pointed at him. Simple awareness that he was a happily married man.

Bikes streamed ahead of him and behind him on the long grinding course. He felt good all the way, taking in fluid periodically under the hot sun. He passed some intermediate riders on the backside of the course, and then began to pass the beginning riders who had started late. Suddenly a bike came surging up beside him. He glanced to one side and almost fell off his bike.

Holly! Grinning with excitement, Bill pointed to a side road up ahead that ascended to a distant point where a wooden platform had been placed to take advantage of the view of green hills that stretched beyond a municipal golf course.

"What are you doing here?" Bill asked when they stopped their bikes, all thoughts of the race forgotten.

"I was waiting for you," she said. "You wanted more adventure."

He still stared at her.

"I've got some good news," she said. "I talked to Dr. Hollawell. I explained our situation. He had warned me about my time involvement at the hospital, so I didn't know how he'd react. But he listened and then said he couldn't promise anything. But he didn't want to lose me. He said there would always be a place at the hospital for me, but he wanted me to stay where I was. He said he understood how I felt, and that my marriage should come first. So he would do some thinking, and if he could work it out some way he would. Maybe even get his executive assistant her own assistant."

Bill kissed her and they made their way back to the road that led to the finish line. As they coasted down the last hill, holding hands, Bill knew that Dr. Hollawell had the reputation of being a good administrator, but if he could work this situation out to everyone's satisfaction, it would be a miracle.

It was.

LOUIS'S LAST BET

I never got to know Louis Reid well during my early months at the paper. Saw his name a lot, one of the paper's best-known political reporters. And in a promo campaign the paper even used his picture on the sides of city buses: "Read Reid—another reason to make the Times-Review *a daily habit."*

Louis was always on the move, digging into the dirt and mire of local and state politics to find buried evidence of corruption and sundry other varieties of dubious shenanigans perpetrated by elected and appointed officials.

He used an extensive network of informers for this, so many office holders automatically fell prey to a severe case of paranoia whenever their receptionist whispered, "Reid would like to talk to you."

Around the office Reid flipped smiles like pancakes, keeping conversation as light as a helium balloon. But his attitude was more serious around Alice Gifford as he plied his own style of courtship.

Alice's desk was near mine. Her quick smile

*was one of the easier things to get used to when
I began my new job. She wrote a daily column,
"Ask Alice," giving advice on all subjects offered her in the form of pleading inquiries or
outraged responses to the slings and arrows of
personal misfortune. We got to know each other
pretty well, at coffee breaks and occasional
lunches. She shared some of her thoughts and
observations about Louis Reid, and eventually I
had enough information to think I might have
found another miracle story.*

Louis Reid was sitting at his desk, his mind drifting ahead to his forthcoming date with Alice, when
the phone rang. He recognized immediately the
scratchy, guttural voice of Ronnie Kildare, the
"chauffeur" of Vice Mayor Pete Milburn.

"We need to talk."

"What about?" Louis asked.

"About thirty minutes—Pearson's." The phone
clicked, and Louis stared at his earpiece. Ronnie
wasn't exactly Mr. Congeniality, but he was able to
get the attention of almost everyone he met. About
six feet six, 260 pounds, he looked more like an enforcer than a chauffeur.

He was a gofer, an enforcer, a chauffeur, an intim-
idator. Call him what you want, but call him "Sir."
Ronnie didn't have much to say unless he was saying
it for Pete Milburn, vice mayor and president of the
Metropolitan Council, the most powerful man in city
government. The mayor was largely a figurehead,
with Pete pulling the strings outside the spotlight.

In some ways Ronnie was a likeable guy. He appeared not very bright, but a lot of that was a front to

give him an edge. He was a lot brighter than he looked. At some level, though, he was almost child-like and naive, someone who responded with appreci-ation for kind words and a friendly gesture. Except when he did something for his boss. Then he was all business, with a pit-bull mentality underneath the sur-face of any outward civility.

Louis ordered two beers and took the bottles with him to a booth at the rear of Pearson's Pub, a place two blocks away from the county courthouse. Ronnie loomed in the front doorway like King Kong looking for Fay Wray. He made his way back to Louis's booth and sat heavily, grabbing his beer and taking a big swallow.

"How are things, Ronnie?" Louis asked.

Ronnie frowned. "Maybe not so good, Lou. Mr. Milburn wants me to give you a message."

Louis nodded. "I'm listening."

"Mr. Milburn thinks that maybe you're getting too friendly with Jerry Pardue."

"I'm a reporter, Ronnie, it's my job to talk to peo-ple in government."

"Talk to some other people."

"Since when is the Planning Commission off-limits?"

Ronnie slowly smiled. He reached into his pocket and pulled out a Kennedy silver dollar. "I appreciate your giving me this coin, Lou. That was real nice."

Louis had known that Ronnie almost worshipped President Kennedy, so he had bought a 1964 Ken-nedy silver dollar, the year when ninety percent of all the Kennedy silver dollars were minted. The remain-ing ten percent—in the years 1965 to 1969, contained only forty percent silver. Only the 1964 coins were one hundred percent silver.

Louis had the coin cleaned and polished and placed in a presentation case before giving it to Ronnie. Now Ronnie put the coin heads up on the table.

"I wouldn't want to hurt you, Lou," he said.

Louis took his own Kennedy silver dollar out of his pocket and placed it on the table, moving it toward Ronnie's coin until they were touching.

"I thought we were friends, Ronnie."

Ronnie picked up his coin and put it back into his pocket.

"I got a job to do, Lou. Don't make it any harder."

"Okay." Louis nodded. "But can you tell me why I shouldn't be friendly with Jerry Pardue?"

Ronnie grinned. "I think you know, Lou. The new landfill is important for the future of the city."

Louis laughed. "You should be in politics, Ronnie."

"A word to the wise, Lou." Ronnie stood.

"Want to flip, Ronnie?"

Ronnie stared at him.

"For the beers." Louis was holding his coin.

"Let's use mine," Ronnie said. "Call it." He flipped.

"Tails," Louis said.

Ronnie caught the coin and slapped it onto the back of his other hand. He held it out to Louis, who nodded.

"You were always lucky, Lou," Ronnie said. "Stay that way."

Louis sat staring after him. Some out-of-state developers were trying to option a big chunk of land near the county line north of the city. The rumor was that they wanted to use it for operating a landfill under contract to the city for a nice fee, but also for use by neighboring counties and communities. Finding space for landfills was getting increasingly difficult as area residents organized and fought against any landfill near their homes. So the issue was volatile, and particularly so since there were two competing sites. A lot of money was at stake, particularly in an operation that served numerous communities. So the usual rumors were floating of payoffs, money passing under the table. At some point in time the Planning Commission would make a recommendation, the council would vote to accept, and the mayor would sign a bill.

In the meantime a good political reporter could find fertile ground for digging up worms even before undertaking an intensive fishing expedition.

Alice appreciated Louis's skills as an investigative reporter, but it was some of his more personal attributes that she gave less than wholehearted approval. Like his penchant for gambling. Even his habit of always saying, "I'll bet you." While some people used this expression as an automatic reflex to fill the space between other thoughts, this often *was* his thought. He meant he would bet you.

He liked to bet, on seemingly just about anything and everything. The elevator comes—want to bet how many people will be on it? A group orders pizza brought in—okay—let's bet on who'll come closer in guessing how long before it arrives. He's was always on top of promoting office betting pools for football and basketball scores.

All this didn't bother his co-workers. They saw it as kind of a job-related activity on his part, since he had made a bundle on a computer gambling game he invented called "Reno Rules." He set it up to use two interfaces—a roulette wheel and a poker game. In roulette, the player could make any bet he wanted, spin the wheel on demand, and watch his earnings increase or vanish, without the pain of an actual Reno visit. With the poker interface, four hands were automatically set up with the player unable to know the cards against him, but able to play his hand by calling for cards, discarding cards, and making bets. The game caught on, and royalties put Louis into an economic bracket that was the envy of all his coworkers. He was such a nice guy that few begrudged him his Mercedes 450 SL or his Brooks Brothers suits.

His eligibility rating was high among the women, but he had never shown an interest in anyone before Alice, causing some to sniff, before Alice came along, that he didn't like women because he already had a mistress—gambling.

His reputation didn't endear him to Alice when she met him. And anyway, he was older—in his forties. Of course, the fact that he somewhat resembled Paul Hogan didn't hurt. When she finally accepted a dinner date, he talked to her about gambling and the theory of probability that shaped its results.

His interest really stemmed from Vietnam. He had served two tours, he said, his voice taking on a tinge of bitterness, back when the war was worth fighting and winning. He had been there in early 1968 during the Tet fighting when the Americans had mopped up on the Viet Cong. Then Congress and the media turned a great American victory into a public relations defeat that started the long road down. But it was in the summer of 1970 when the Americans entered Cambodia to clean out Cong bases that Louis first started thinking about the theory of probability.

Ken Myers, a fairly new guy in his platoon, and he

were crouched in a ditch outside a small village that was reported to contain a large cache of arms and ammunition. It was just before dawn. The setting seemed peaceful. Ken reached into his pocket and pulled out a coin, and flipped it. Then he flipped it again, and again. And a fourth time.

"What are you doing?" Louis asked in a low voice.

"I'm flipping my lucky coin. If it comes up heads, we'll be okay."

He flipped again.

"Why do you keep flipping it?" Louis's whisper was tense as he waited for the order to attack.

"It keeps coming up tails."

Louis grabbed the coin in mid-air and looked at it. A Kennedy silver dollar.

"Your lucky coin?"

Ken nodded.

"This guy wasn't lucky," Louis said.

Ken took the coin back and was about to flip it again when their sergeant motioned them forward. Just as they began movement grenades went off and machine gun bullets ripped at them. An ambush—and when it was over the whole village was a landfill of severed limbs and mangled bodies. The Cong had fled, but not before inflicting a high number of casualties. One casualty was Ken, and beside him on the ground was the coin he had not flipped that final time.

They found no cache of arms in the village.

Louis didn't dwell on the carnage of the scene to Alice, but he described how he picked up Ken's coin and flipped it, and wondered about it. He flipped the coin over and over that day, watching the heads and tails accumulate seemingly with no governing law. He thought about the randomness of the way the coin tuned up, and the randomness of the way some men die and some men live in battle. Was there some underlying principle or law that governed chance? Why had Ken's coin come up tails so many times in succession? What were the odds of that happening, and why did it happen at that particular time?

Louis showed her a coin. "That's it," he said. "Ken's silver dollar."

She looked closely at it. An ordinary coin. She handed it back.

Louis went on to describe how—when he got back—he read all the articles and books he could find on probability theory. He learned that the chance of two independent events happening is equal to the product of the two separate probabilities. The odds on tossing tails once is two to one against. The odds of tossing tails twice in a row is four to one against. Four flips, like Ken had made, and the odds were sixteen to one it wouldn't happen.

Louis said he remembered how much his parents had liked bridge. Probability theory taught him the odds against any one person receiving a complete suit in the deal was almost 160 billion to one. Yet about one report each year is made of such a "perfect deal," something that clearly shouldn't happen that frequently.

Of course, Louis grinned, "Pranks, deception, and deceit have been known to contribute their support to unusual claims about chance.

"When it comes to chance, better stick to probability theory," Louis said.

"Take roulette," he went on, "one of my two interfaces in 'Reno Rules.' Roulette is no gamble for the house. There are thirty-six slots plus zero and often a double zero. So the individual should have odds of one chance in thirty-eight to hit—right?"

She nodded.

"Wrong," he said. "The house only gives odds of thirty-five to one whereas there are thirty-eight options. This means the house insures itself a built-in long-term advantage of more than five percent on turnover. This advantage is nothing but a license to rob the poor guy who thinks he's getting a fair shake at roulette.

"In 'Reno Rules' I give my players an honest game. I took away the five percent advantage for the house. A player may not realize it, but he'll win more often in my game than he could in Reno or Vegas.

"Hey," he said suddenly, "let's order." He gestured to the server, who had stayed discreetly away while his patrons seemed to be enthusiastically conversing.

After they ordered—Louis went for the Swiss steak, while Alice chose veal parmesan and barely got settled back in her chair before Louis asked her a question.

"Do you play poker?"

She shook her head.

"You've seen movies where the hero is playing for high stakes, and everything comes down to the final hand? The bad guy has a terrific hand, maybe a straight, thereby bucking the odds of 254 to one against having it, and the hero then comes in with a full house, bucking odds of 693 to one. Or the one I really like is when the bad guy comes up with a straight flush—thinking he's won it all—and he should, because the odds for getting a straight flush is one chance in 72,192. But no—the hero lays out a royal flush to take the pot. The odds against getting a royal flush are 649,739 to one."

She looked at him with amazement. "You went to the trouble to memorize all that?"

"Games of chance are fascinating. Everything hinges on probability theory. The more you understand about the theory, the better off you are. And you know what probability theory can do better than anything else?"

"What?"

"Help keep people from being addicted to gambling."

She smiled. "You mean you're not addicted?"

"Gambling's a hobby," he said. "Well—more than a hobby if you consider that 'Reno Rules' gives me most of my income. My other gambling is strictly small stakes, even if some people consider me some kind of an expert."

"You certainly don't discourage the idea that you like to gamble."

"I encourage small bets because they add a little excitement and spice to an otherwise drab and routine day."

She shook her head. "Let me tell you about my father. I haven't told anyone this since I moved here, and I'm not sure why I'm telling you. But maybe you'll understand why I don't like to be around any kind of gambling—even small bets and 'heads we will, tails we won't.'

"My father was a wonderful man, owned a watch repair shop in an old office building in the downtown business district. As malls proliferated and businesses left downtown, so did customers. He couldn't afford to go into a mall, and was hurting financially. One of his customers was a bookie. You can figure out the rest."

Louis waited. Alice continued, "He probably began thinking one big win could rescue him. But he continued until he was hopelessly in debt. And it wasn't just horse races. Card games, whatever he could find. He was like a person who diets and loses control and develops anorexia. We got him in to see a doctor and came away with words like 'obsessive-compulsive neuroses.' But nothing helped, and finally he killed himself."

"I'm sorry," Louis said.

"And you want to hear the final irony?" she asked. "Until the end he never quit gambling. When we found him the revolver contained no bullets."

"You mean—?"

She nodded. "Russian roulette."

They ate a little, then she looked at him. "Do you really think if people understood probability theory the logic of the odds would keep them from being willing to risk the farm or their life's savings on one turn of the wheel or throw of the dice or one draw of the card?"

He nodded. "Probability theory proves that any high-stakes gambling is a fool's bet."

"I've got news for you," she said, "what happened to my father taught me that gambling is driven by emotions, not logic. And sometimes the emotions get sick, which makes gambling an even bigger problem."

He grew silent then, and they got down to serious eating. He knew she was right about the power of emotions. She saw that every day as she answered letters from people in the throes of emotion, many whose emotions had driven them to rash acts. He recognized that emotion was driving him—but not to commit a rash act. He figured that dating Alice was probably the most logical thing he had done in his life.

At home that night Alice thought back on the evening and was a little surprised at her reaction—she'd had a good time. Probability theory would doubtless decree that she would never have an interest in Louis Reid. He almost qualified as being from an older generation—she had trouble with that thought—and she had learned enough about his attitudes to know he was not fully in tune with her modern feminist proclivities. But his demeanor was so relentlessly upbeat, so totally focused on what was happening now, that he seemed impossibly young, younger than most of her contemporaries.

She knew his job must sometimes carry him into dark corners of local politics where he sometimes saw raw examples of greed and corruption. But she felt no cynicism in him that she assumed many reporters in his world would find endemic. The fact that Louis could have lived through the terrible experiences of Vietnam and now work where he did without losing his innate sense of optimism, might mean that this guy was special.

She thought of what advice she would give herself in her column "Ask Alice": "Keep an open mind and take a chance, but don't bet your future on the gambler."

One last word echoed in her mind as she went to sleep: "Yet."

But as the days went by Alice found it harder and harder not to place a bet on the gambler. His smiles kept coming, the irrepressible optimistic confidence he exuded in her presence regarding their ultimate relationship was almost overwhelming.

On their dates she often asked herself, What's not

to like? A leathery hunk of a man who looks at her like she's state-of-the-art female. What's bad about a man with a sense of humor that can smooth out the wrinkles in the garment of frustrations she sometimes found herself wearing. Antidote extraordinaire for PMS.

She still didn't like the idea of his gambling—even "small stakes," as he described it. That was his business. He wasn't hurting anyone. She told herself that she was silly. Why should what he did bother her? He wasn't like her father in any way.

On his part, Louis always remembered the story about her father, and tried to keep any references to gambling out of his conversation. Particularly, he kept his silver dollar in his pocket, after one time when they were in his car waiting at a stop light. He took his dollar out of his pocket and suddenly flipped it in the air and at the same time said, "Heads, that red Beemer at the light goes right, tails it goes left." She had looked at him with her innocent blue eyes and asked, "What if it goes straight?"

The landfill story had heated up at the council meeting the previous Tuesday night. A vote was scheduled for accepting or rejecting the recommendation of the Public Works Department that the city contract with the out-of-state Amalgamated Land Use Company as the operator of a new landfill to be located on a specified block of property that butted against a section of the county line north of the city. Said operator would lease said property for a period of fifty years from Green Acres Corporation, property owner.

Louis had expected the vote to be favorable without much dissent. Talk was that the skids had been greased, and Louis figured the city boys in on the deal would now look forward to a regular piece of the ongoing action. But before the vote Vice Mayor Pete Milburn called on Murray King from the Solid Waste Division of the Public Works Department to make a report. Murray appeared a little nervous, but soon picked up steam as he related how further study by his division showed the city could save money if it continued to operate its own landfill. New calculations based on a parade of statistics related to employee salaries, transportation, and equipment operating budgets soon befuddled a number of council members who obviously had no prior warning of this new development. A motion was made to accept the new recommendation of the Public Works Department, reject the independent out-of-state company, and ask the Public Works Department to present a new recommendation for the site of the new landfill, since now there were two other locations to be considered.

So what was the deal? Louis picked up a phone and called Jerry Pardue in the Planning Commission, but Jerry sounded harried and said he couldn't talk. Louis hung up, thinking he'd call Jerry at home tonight. Then his own phone rang, and Louis recognized the voice of an old poker-playing buddy who was one of his sources into the inner workings of the council.

"Hey, Louis, how about a game of pool?" Fred Abrams was a lawyer who served as council person from the seventeenth district. They often met at Paul's Billiards whenever either one wanted to initiate a conference with the other.

"Sure thing, Fred."

"In an hour?" Fred asked.

"See you there," Louis answered.

Pocket billiards was Louis's favorite kind of pool. He enjoyed both Chicago and pyramid pool, but he liked hearing the payoff to a good shot—the solid chunk into the called pocket. For that reason he did not care much for American billiards.

He and Fred had discovered that the most private place for a conversation was in a setting of movement, where no one thought of confidential words being passed.

Louis broke first, slightly to the right of the foot spot. Two balls dropped. He started a run that went to eight. Then Fred took over.

"What's the deal on the landfill vote?" Louis asked.

"I don't know. The talk was that a lot of people were going to be happy after the vote."

"So what's going on?"

"Maybe I know someone who can tell you," Fred said, finishing up the fifteen balls. This time he broke, and started another run.

"Ralph Watson called me," Fred said. "He knows we're friends, and he wanted me to contact you and let you know he wanted to talk to you."

Fred finally missed, and Louis set up the shot, calling for the seven ball in the far corner. He felt a hum of excitement as he considered the possibilities of Ralph Watson, an administrative assistant to Vice Mayor Pete Milburn.

"One thing," Fred added after a few moments, "he said not to call him at the office. He said he'd call you at home tonight."

On his way back to the office Louis figured that he had a more interesting person to talk to tonight than Jerry Pardue.

After an early dinner he dropped Alice off at home early, saying he was expecting a phone call. She looked disappointed.

The call came at about eighty-thirty. Ralph's voice

sounded low. "Can you speak louder?" Louis asked, wondering if this were going to be the local version of *Deep Throat*.

"I want us to talk."

"Name it," Louis said.

"You know where the Starlite Lounge is?"

Louis knew. A roadhouse on Highway 65, south of town.

"Go there. I'll call you and tell you where to go."

"It will take me thirty minutes," Louis said.

What a buildup, he thought, driving. Super spy stuff. This had better be good or he would charge Ralph for mileage.

A lot of smoke and voices and honky-tonk music filled the air as he sat in a booth near the wall phone. After five minutes the phone rang, and the bartender answered it. Louis rose and moved close, gesturing to himself when the bartender looked around.

"Are you Louis Reid?"

Louis nodded, and the bartender handed him the phone. Again the low voice. "Ride on out of town over the hill and after two miles you'll come to a long gravel driveway that goes to a farm house. I'll be waiting in my car."

Louis followed the directions and came to a dark car. He pulled into the driveway and shut off his lights. He saw no one. He got out of his car and moved to the other car, looking in. No one.

Okay, Louis thought. What have we got here?

"Boo!"

The word came from right behind him and in one second Louis gained fifty new gray hairs and lost three years from his life expectancy.

"Great day, Ralph!" Louis exclaimed. "Did you get me out here to scare me to death?"

"Sorry," Ralph said, "I haven't been laughing much lately and I couldn't resist."

For the first time Louis thought he might end up liking Ralph a little.

"What have you got?" Louis asked.

"I want my name kept out of it."

"Don't we all."

"Look, I'll give you some information. But you've got to also get it from another source. Then later if any question comes up about where you got information it can be explained so I'm kept clear."

"I always get two sources anyway."

"Yeah," Ralph said, "you've got a good reputation. That's why I came to you."

"So let's hear it."

"You know about Green Acres Corporation?"

"Sure. They own the landfill property."

"Do you know who owns Green Acres?"

"Two brothers—George and Leon Nichols. They can't be happy about the council's vote."

"Green Acres has a lot of silent partners, and they're not as unhappy as you think."

"What do you mean?" Louis asked.

"They've got a better use for the property than leasing it to an out-of-state landfill operator."

Louis's interest level was rising like a thermometer responding to fever.

"Like what?"

"A shopping mall. Land development for businesses, residences, the whole banana."

"You're kidding," Louis said. "There's nothing out there. Not even access."

Ralph was silent.

"Wait a minute," Louis said. "You're saying these

guys have advance knowledge so they can speculate on a land deal?"

Ralph still said nothing.

"We're talking about big-time collusion at the state level."

"We're also talking about big-time jail sentences when this gets out," Ralph said. Then he added, "With early publicity this whole thing can be stopped before anyone gets hurt."

"How come you're the boy scout?" Louis asked.

"Too many people are in on it. Sooner or later someone will talk, and with plea bargains turn evidence that might reach even to hangers-on like me. I'm no insider in the deal, but I'm standing too close to those who are. They get tarred, I'll feel the bristles of the brush, too."

Ralph shook his head. "I've worked for Pete Milburn for years, and I've gone along with a lot of things. But he never understood about my wife. Edith was a Christian, Mr. Reid. She was honest and she wanted me to be. Pete used to kid me about my wife's beliefs. I would sometimes go to church with her and Pete would make jokes about my church-going. When she died of breast cancer last year Pete sent the biggest bouquet of flowers at the funeral. He told me what a wonderful example she was as a faithful church member, but I knew how he really felt, and his hypocrisy was worse than if he had flat out insulted her. I'm tired of working for him."

"Well, Ralph," Louis said, "it seems to me you're getting close to having a reason to send out your resume."

"I needed the job when Edith was sick to help pay medical bills. But the last night in the hospital room before Edith died she held my hand and said God was watching over her, that she could feel God was waiting for her. She said we were always close to heaven, and should conduct ourselves on Earth so we would have nothing to be ashamed of when we get to heaven."

Ralph cleared his throat. "I never thought about God, Mr. Reid. I let Edith carry faith for both of us. But it doesn't work that way. I'm going to be seeing Edith soon, and she'll know what I've done since she's been away. I've got to do what she would want me to do." Ralph lowered his head and began to cry.

Louis was uncomfortable, not knowing what to say. At the same time he marveled at human nature. Ralph was a veteran of local politics, knew the ins and outs of what went on in many corridors of the mighty. Had seen deals made that smelled worse than Baker's Fish Market on an August afternoon. Yet when human thought tries to embrace the most important things in life to give some sense of what is most meaningful, the greatest comfort comes from voicing words that affirm the reality of heaven and the closeness of God, the same words that politicians working their deals laugh at when they see them printed in a Sunday school leaflet that sells at fifty cents for a hundred copies.

For himself, Louis knew he still had a lot of digging to do, but he had a contact in the office of the state district attorney general, and also in the investigations section of the state commerce department. And one thing he could do right away—float a few of the old faithful "rumor as source" articles that don't prove anything but sure do stir the pot.

Louis held out his hand. "Thanks, Ralph. I'll keep your name out of it in the paper. But sooner or later, you may be called to testify."

"I know," Ralph said. "Mr. Milburn let me get

close not because he liked me, but because he thought I'd be afraid to do anything that would threaten him. I'm not afraid anymore."

Louis's first article in the series he eventually wrote began like this:

"Rumors abound in town of a windfall that might come to certain individuals who were smart enough to know that where there is an exit from an interstate, there is great potential reward for those who invest in nearby land. At this point the rumors only raise questions, not give answers.

"One question: Does anyone have advance knowledge of where an exit from an interstate might be built in this county?"

Several departments at the state level had people ferreting out information and interviewing probable suspects. Heat generated a squirming of the worms. Louis received death threats via phone and fax and mail. His friend in the state district attorney general's office thought it might be good if he wore a wire and kept in contact with an undercover operative assigned to follow him around for awhile.

During all this time, Alice tried to be understanding, but it was difficult, because by this time she had pushed all her chips on the table and bet her heart on the gambler.

"This will soon be over," Louis assured her.

Then late one afternoon he got a phone call from someone who wanted to meet him and give him a hot tip that would blow the roof off the mayor's office and other assorted offices including that of the vice mayor. The voice called for Louis to come alone to the old warehouse area on the riverfront near First Avenue South. A trap? Maybe, and maybe not.

As Louis drove he took comfort in knowing that Jeff Storey was following him two blocks back, and in radio contact.

"This area is a great place for an ambush," Jeff's voice came over his speaker. Louis was thinking the same thing.

He pulled up in front of a warehouse where he saw a parked car. He got out and examined the car. No one there. Shades of Ralph Watson. Was someone about to jump out and say "Boo?"

He heard a sudden screech of tires coming up behind him. This was worse than a boo, because getting out of the car was big Ronnie Kildare with two other guys who looked like they were auditioning for *Gorillas in the Mist*.

"I'm sorry, Lou," Ronnie said, fitting some brass knuckles onto his fingers, "I got to hurt you a little." Thank goodness Jeff was coming.

"Ronnie, let's think about this," urged Louis.

"I warned you, Lou. Didn't I warn you?"

Louis nodded. Where was Jeff?

Ronnie moved closer, and the other two closed in from either side.

The siren, Jeff, he thought. Come in with siren roaring!

No Jeff. Only Ronnie, the smiling giant.

"I hate to do this. But I warned you."

"Wait—!" Louis yelled.

"It won't last long, Louis. I'll just work on your kidneys a little. You may bleed a few days when you go to the bathroom. But it will get all right. I know how hard to hit. You'll see."

The two men grabbed his arms. "Wait. Ronnie, let's make a bet."

"Aw, Lou, that ain't goin' to help you," Ronnie said.

"The Kennedy dollar. Flip it. If it comes up my way you don't hit me."

Ronnie grinned. "Okay, Lou. We'll bet. But we'll play with my dollar." He pulled the coin out of his pocket.

"The only thing is," Ronnie said, "if it comes up your way I flip again. And I keep flipping until it comes up right."

"I'll take heads," Louis said.

"You'll take tails," Ronnie said. He flipped the coin and let it hit the ground.

"You win, Lou," Ronnie said, picking up the coin. "Tails."

He flipped again. "You're a lucky man, Lou. Tails again."

Where was Jeff?

The coin was in the air again. "I'll be doggone," Ronnie said. "Three tails in a row."

"You beat everybody for luck." Ronnie picked up the coin. "I'm getting tired of this game."

"Remember the bet. You can't hit me when it comes up tails."

Another toss, and now Louis had one chance in sixteen of getting tails. The coin hit the ground. Louis breathed again. Tails.

Then came the blaring sound of a siren as Jeff braked to a stop. He jumped out of the car pointing a gun.

"Hands up!" he yelled.

Ronnie held up his hands. "We haven't done anything. We don't have any guns. We're just having a conversation." He looked at Louis and smiled. "You really are lucky, aren't you, Lou?"

"And if I suddenly get unlucky, the cops will know where to come and make someone else unlucky."

Ronnie nodded. "Four tails in a row," he muttered as he got into the car. "Who would have believed it?"

Louis watched them drive away. There was still a lot of work to do before Pete Milburn ended up unlucky. But somehow he felt that day was coming.

"I'm sorry," he said. "A funeral procession held me up at the corner of Eighth and Broad."

Louis shook his head. "That was almost my funeral."

It took three more months before the investigation wrapped up. And then the trial began. Louis knew that many more months would go by before justice flipped a heads or a tails.

But for Alice justice came one evening as they walked in Riverside Park and stopped at a level area near the water. The river was unusually calm, the surface almost as smooth as a lake. The sun was setting and sent a golden path across the water straight at them.

"Beautiful," Alice said. "I wish we could walk on that."

Louis reached into his pocket and brought out his silver dollar.

"What are you going to do with that?" she asked.

"I don't need this anymore. But it's been a faithful friend, and it deserves its chance to find its own golden destiny."

He whipped his arm around and the dollar soared, spinning over the water in line with the path of light until it hit, skipped, and skipped again until the fourth time it disappeared forever in the reflection of the setting sun.

THE LAST ANGRY NERD

I heard about Wayne Murphy when a good friend, the pastor of the Vine Street Presbyterian Church, called me and told me about a boy in his church who had recently won third place in a national competition called, "The Christopher Science Talent Search." As he explained, this competition was open to all high school students who planned and developed a science project. College scholarships were given to the winners.

The pastor explained that Wayne Murphy had grown up in the church, and the congregation was proud of him. He had always been shy, and the pastor hoped this new recognition might give him more self-confidence. The pastor wondered if I might feature Wayne or at least reference him in an article.

I said I would talk to Wayne, and the pastor gave me his phone number. Wayne was reluctant at first, but he finally agreed to meet me.

As we talked I began to wonder about Wayne's supposed lack of self-confidence. He certainly had a lot to feel confident about. He was obviously

*very bright, without any of the pseudo-intellectual
arrogance that sometimes bright people project as
a sign of their superiority to the common herd.*

*Wayne's third-place award of a fifteen-
thousand-dollar scholarship resulted from a
research project showing how different teaching methods in two sixth-grade classes affected
students' comprehension.*

*I found myself drawn to Wayne, and I didn't
want to lose track of him. So that summer we
got together for lunch a number of times and he
began to open up about his personal life. He introduced me to someone else, and her story became part of his. I decided that what I heard
and inferred might qualify as one of my miracle
stories.*

Maybe he was a sucker for girls with big noses. In
his lifetime Wayne Murphy had fallen for two girls
with big noses. Miss Helen Farraway was his teacher
in the second grade, and his crush was bigger than an
iceberg's bottom half.

Miss Farraway's nose was big, but her smile lit up
the corner of every room she entered. And Wayne
thought she had a special smile just for him, that
somehow he and Miss Farraway had a secret relationship that went far deeper than what she felt for any
other kids in class. He hung around her every chance
he got. And then one day not long before a spring
day when the entire grade school spent their annual
picnic day in the country to celebrate another year's
drawing to a close, as the teachers kept watch over
their respective flocks, Wayne overheard Miss
Farraway tell another teacher that she was getting

married and would not be back at the school next year.

The yelling and the laughter of the other kids suddenly lost their meaning, and the world seemed an empty place. The thought was almost unbearable that Miss Farraway wouldn't be around anymore, that she'd be gone forever.

The rest of that day Wayne didn't leave Miss Farraway's side and was content to hold her hand as much as she would let him.

Now his feelings were a little different. He was ten years older, and the girl of his dreams, Dawn Lawrence, was an auburn-haired, dark-skinned girl with a lazy smile and the best legs that ever transported any high school senior.

Another thing that caught him was her hair. She wore it long and had a way of moving her head so that he always imagined how soft her hair would feel to touch. Her smile framed perfect teeth, and the smile came often. Her skin was naturally very dark, so that all winter she seemed to have a terrific tan. About her nose, well, it was a little long with a thin bridge that featured a small hook. A Roman nose, or maybe that of an Indian warrior as seen in profile looking toward a distant range of mountains.

Her nose bothered Wayne not at all. He would not have changed a centimeter of it, because it was simply a part of her. In fact, he thought it was beautiful.

But he had never told her of his feelings. Like he had done with Miss Farraway, he simply tried to stay as close to her as possible, freeing his desires and dreams to live only in a world of his secret fantasy.

Wayne was what many adults would call an increasingly rare specimen in the teenage population of America—a "brain." He liked to study. He wanted to learn things where he had no previous knowledge. Naturally, his teachers had always adopted him as their "shining example" and "hope for the future," which did much to isolate him from the ordinary life and concerns of the other students, who also pigeon-holed him as an "apple polisher." His own inclination built the rest of the fortification that kept him isolated. His natural interests did not embrace what he considered the mundane and superficial concerns that monopolized the conversation of many of his peers.

So in addition to "brain," Wayne was "nerd" to his classmates, a term that automatically consigned him to irrelevant creaturehood as far as girls were concerned.

Dawn Lawrence stared at herself in the mirror. Why did her mother always complain about her clothes? What's so bad about a leather skirt and vest, yellow scarf, black boots and pantyhose, and brass chain belt?

Her parents didn't get it. She didn't want to dress like everyone else. She had been like everybody else all her life. Dressing like everybody else, doing the expected thing, like going to church every Sunday.

Except for one Sunday, when she rode to church on Howie's motorcycle. Okay, so the bike was a little noisy coming into the parking lot. Big deal.

At least she had gotten Howie to come to church that day. Her parents were always complaining about Howie. Even when they weren't actually talking about Howie their attitude made clear what they were thinking.

Howie didn't live on the right side of town. His parents were not members of the Crestfield Country Club. Howie was not one who would ever apply for medical school. But Howie was a lot more fun than most of her socially acceptable friends. And she was old enough to choose friends who were different—like Howie and Sally Coggins.

Sally was another friend who was high on her parents' clucking meter. Sally liked to wear leather, too, accessorizing with loud contrasting colors and heavy metal jewelry.

One time Dawn's mother had sniffed about Sally's "abominable" taste, and Dawn had smiled, knowing the barb was really aimed at her.

Howie stopped the bike in front of Dawn's house and felt the weight on the seat shift as Dawn got off.

"Aw, don't go to the library," he said, "not tonight. Let's go to the Green Wall."

"I can't," she said. "I've got to work with Wayne on our research paper."

"It's Friday night."

"Our paper's due next week."

"Let Nerdville write it."

"We're supposed to work on it together. I told you, we work together in chem lab, and the teacher assigned the paper to both of us. We can get extra credit. And believe me," she said, "I need all the extra credit I can get in chemistry."

"Mr. Brain will end up writing it anyway. Just put your name on it."

"Look, Howie," Dawn patiently explained, "we have to read a lot of articles. We'll divide up and each write notes and the bibliographic references, and then put everything together."

"And the nerd will write it."

"He'll write the draft," she admitted, "but I'll read it and offer suggestions. It will be our work."

"Come on, Babe," he pled, "the Green Wall. Dead Reverie is playing tonight."

"Sorry," she said, and turned to walk away.

"I'll call you tomorrow," he yelled after her. She gave a quick wave.

He watched her walk all the way to the house. The place was two stories with two tall columns and a wide portico, with a circular granite driveway in front. He never took the bike up the drive to let her off at the house because of her parents' express wishes.

At times like this he felt something he would never admit, even to himself—a shadow of doubt. His old man on a good year might clear fifty thousand, and he doubted he'd ever do better. So what was he doing dreaming of some chick who lives in a place like this and whose father owns some kind of an appraiser outfit?

Well, he thought as he gunned the motor, at least he wasn't as pathetic as that Murphy creep who walks around with his nose stuck in a book.

The tires squealed as he accelerated away, leaving behind loose gravel and the thoughts that made him uncomfortable.

That night Wayne swung into the Lawrence driveway with a surge of enthusiasm. Dawn had called him and asked him to pick her up. Her car wouldn't start. He knocked on the door and wished he were coming for a regular date. But at least this was better than the normal "see you at the library" gig.

She appeared wearing a tan shirtwaist dress that did nothing to hide those knockout legs. He did his best to keep from staring.

"Thanks for picking me up," she said, getting into the car. "A battery boost wouldn't start it. I think it's the carburetor."

After a few moments he said hesitantly, "I like your dress."

She smiled. "My mother gave this to me on my last birthday. I've never worn it much. Her idea of clothes and mine are not identical twins."

He made no comment. She glanced at him. "Do you have any problems with your parents?"

"Not really," he said. "Why do you ask?"

She smiled. "You seem like someone who would never give his parents any trouble."

"Why do you think that?"

"Because," she shrugged, "you seem so—"

"Dull?" he filled in.

"No. Settled. Well adjusted."

"That's me. Well adjusted," he said drily.

She looked curiously at him.

"Aren't you?" she asked.

"You mean because I don't ride a motorcycle or wear an earring or smoke cigarettes?"

"I don't mean that," she said. "I've just been a little curious about you. Everyone knows you'll be valedictorian, and no one knows much about you."

"I'm not—real comfortable meeting people."

"That sounds strange with your interest in psychology."

"How did you know about my interest in psychology?"

"The school assembly, remember? When the principal announced you were a semifinalist in the Christopher Science Talent Search. Incidentally, I hope you win."

"I'll be happy to win any of the scholarships," he said. Then he added, "Maybe my problem is a reason why I like psychology."

"So have you figured out your problem?" she smiled. "By the way, what is your problem?"

"Can't you tell?" he asked. "I'm slightly introverted."

"What's wrong with that?"

"Nothing, if you feel good about yourself. But sometimes when I don't say what's on my mind then later I kick myself."

"I hope you don't think I'm prying," she said, "but a lot of kids are curious about you."

He laughed, "Most of them couldn't care less."

"That isn't true," she said.

"They think I'm a nerd."

"Some do," she admitted, "but a lot of them are envious of how well you do in school."

He swallowed hard. Maybe this was the time to say what he was thinking, he thought. "You know about the Science Club?" he asked.

"Sure," she said. "Aren't you a member?"

He nodded. "A couple of the members are spelunkers," he said. "Two weeks from Saturday the club is going to Crawford's Cave in Rutherford County. It's a big cave, not well developed yet. We're going to spend all day exploring it."

"Sounds like fun," she said.

"I—" he sputtered, "—I wondered if you would like to go?"

She shook her head. "I'm sorry. I told Howie I'd go with him to Crawfordville that day."

"Crawfordville? You mean for Bike Day?"

She was surprised. "You know about that? Howie's riding in the open moto-cross race."

"I'm surprised you'd be interested in Bike Day."

"Howie says all the activities will be under strict control. Nothing wild."

"He's right about that," Wayne said. "The Metro Bike Club keeps strict rules. Full cooperation is given by the police in any town selected by the club. The fact is, the town knows the guys will be spending a lot of money, and the merchants are glad to see the bikers. I went last year with my brother when it was held in Martin's Landing. Had a good time, but it still doesn't seem like something you'd enjoy. You have to like bikes to get really involved in the activities."

"I like bikes," she said.

"And you like Howie," he thought, beginning to feel like a turtle as he sensed his head retracting into its shell.

At the library they worked for a couple of hours, pulling books and making notes. She gave him some sheets of paper and he put them into his notebook.

"I'll get this typed up," he said, "and we can go over the draft one night next week."

"Fine," she said. "Call me. Any night's okay."

At that moment Sally Coggins walked up to their table. "Aren't you through working yet?" she asked Dawn. "I came to rescue you."

"We just finished," Dawn said. "Say hello to Wayne."

Sally nodded at him and looked quickly back at Dawn.

"I didn't see your car in the parking lot."

"My car wouldn't start. Wayne brought me."

"I'll take you home," Sally said, "after we go to Barkey's."

"I'll take you home," Wayne broke in.

Dawn looked at him, "Do you want to go to Barkey's?"

"Sure," Wayne said. Sally looked at him like he

had crawled out of a rotten log. He smiled sweetly. He had never liked Sally.

Barkey's was a pizza place, and Wayne felt a little uncomfortable sitting in the middle of a fast-talking group of girls who seemed to communicate in a foreign language. When he and Dawn and Sally had entered, Dawn and Sally immediately saw a table with three other girls, and joined them with the excitement of not having seen them for two centuries. Although Wayne sat there saying nothing and feeling like a stranger in a strange land, Sally suddenly turned to him and said loudly, "Wayne has been working at the library with Dawn on a research paper." She batted her eyes.

"What is the paper about, Wayne?" she asked.

"It's about plastics," Wayne said.

"Plastics. How nice," Sally said, glancing knowingly at the other girls.

"That sounds fascinating," she added.

"Actually," Wayne said, "it's about the history of polymerization."

"Polymer who?" Sally said, and the other girls giggled.

"Polymerization is the combination of small molecules into long chains of polymers to create plastics," Wayne said.

Jan reached into her pocket and pulled out a comb. "Like this?"

Wayne nodded. "Right. The process became important in the 1930s and resulted in a number of important plastics in wide use today."

"Whatever," Sally said, and ran her comb through Wayne's hair, streaming it over his forehead.

"Hey!"

Sally ignored him and started talking to the girls.

"Did any of you see that new tattoo Eddie Brewer got on his left shoulder?"

Wayne heard the sound of a motorcycle and glanced out the window beside their booth toward the parking lot. He saw Howie dismount from his bike.

"There's Howie," Sally said. The girls turned toward the door as Howie entered and came their way.

"Howie, sit by me." Sally's voice could have been put to music. She patted the seat. He slid in beside her.

"Hello, Sal," he said. "You been studying at the library, like certain other people?"

She laughed. "I've got better things to do."

"Don't we all," he said, looking at Dawn. "Did you and Einstein get finished with your project?"

"Most of it," she said.

Howie nodded. "I was hoping I might find you here. I'll take you home."

"Wayne is taking me home," Dawn said.

"Oh?" said Wayne, looking at Howie, then back at Dawn.

"Maybe he doesn't want to take you home," Howie said. "Maybe he'd rather I take you home."

"I'm taking Dawn home," Wayne said in a soft voice.

"Is that what you really want?" Howie asked Dawn. "Do you want the brain tumor to take you home?"

"Wayne will take me home," Dawn said evenly.

"You can take me home, Howie," the musical voice of Sally was like a caress.

Howie ignored her and stood up abruptly. "I'll see you." He left, legged-over his bike, and bolted from the parking lot.

"I'm sorry Howie was so rude to you tonight," Dawn said later in the car.

Wayne smiled. "Maybe he's a little jealous."

"Jealous of you?" she laughed. "That's crazy."

"You're right," Wayne said drily. "No one should be jealous of me. Pretty presumptuous of me."

She frowned. "I didn't mean anything by that."

"I'm sorry," he said. "I didn't mean anything, either. Just making conversation."

Wayne added, "Howie would probably be jealous of any guy who only wanted to ask you directions to the post office."

She shook her head. "I've made it clear to him about that. We're not going steady, and he doesn't own me. I go out with him because he's fun, and if he stops being fun, that's it."

Wayne first noticed the light behind him about four blocks from her home. Then the light in the rearview mirror rapidly got bigger.

"Looks like we have company," he said.

She looked behind, just as the bike roared up on her side of the car. Howie's head stayed near her window as they rolled side by side.

"You're too near the curb, Howie," Dawn yelled, motioning him back. He cut his speed and dropped behind the car and gunned around the other side and passed to the front and began to weave back and forth in the front headlights. Then once again he dropped behind.

"He isn't being fun this way," Dawn said through tight lips. Now the bike sped up to tailgate the car, and then dropped back. Howie repeated this maneuver over and over.

"He may be slightly jealous," Wayne opined right before slamming on his brakes. Then he goosed the accelerator and the car jumped ahead. But Wayne heard the sound of screeching brakes behind him as Howie braked and then twisted the handlebars, sending his bike over the curb. The bump parted him from the seat and he rose over the handlebars and landed hard on the far side of the sidewalk. Wayne pulled up at the curb and got out. Dawn ran over to Howie and bent down. "Are you all right?"

Howie groggily got to his feet and yelled at Wayne. "Why did you put your brakes on? I almost ran into you!"

"That was to tell you to quit playing around."

"I was just having a little fun."

"What you were doing was dangerous."

"You were acting like a jerk, Howie," Dawn said.

He stared at her, fury building in his eyes. He turned to Wayne. "Maybe you need to learn what danger is." He put his hand on Wayne's chest and pushed hard.

"Howie!" Dawn grabbed at Howie's arm. He jerked away and took a step toward Wayne. His first blow doubled Wayne over, and then he brought up a right uppercut that leveled Wayne to the ground.

"You're acting crazy!" Dawn exclaimed and bent down over Wayne, helping him sit up. She turned to face Howie.

"Get out of here. I don't want to see you again."

He stared at her and his expression changed.

"I'm sorry," he said.

"Just go," she said.

Finally he muttered, "It was his fault." He slowly got his bike upright, pressed the starter button, and left.

Dawn helped Wayne stand. "Your face looks bad," she said. "Does it hurt a lot?"

"Only when I talk."

"Want me to drive?" she asked. "Maybe I ought to drive you home."

"I can make it," he said.

At her place, before she got out of the car, she suddenly laughed. "Maybe our research will tell us how you can get a plastic jaw."

"That would be better than a glass jaw," he said.

"Well," she said, "now that I won't be going to Bike Day with Howie, would you still like me to go spelunking?"

"I don't think so," Wayne said.

"Oh?" she said in a small voice, plainly surprised.

"I've got a better idea for that day," Wayne said. "I want you to go with me to Bike Day."

"You're kidding."

He shook his head. "Will you go with me?"

"Howie will be there," she said.

"So?"

"So I don't want to watch him act like a jerk anymore."

"I promise," he said, "to avoid trouble with him."

She stared at him. "Maybe the kids at school are wrong about you. Maybe you're not so bright."

"Will you go with me?"

"I don't know why I would go with you. But maybe I'm not very bright, either. Okay, I'll go."

"Great," Wayne said. "And by the way, we'll go on one of my brother's bikes."

She was surprised. "I didn't know you could ride a bike."

"At my house that's the only way to stay alive. My brother's a fanatic—always working on bikes. I like cars better, but I ride his bikes for fun."

Dawn watched the car until it disappeared. She

wondered what had happened to that shy, quiet boy who always kept to himself, who seemed to have no interest in high school other than pulling straight A's. Obviously he had no interest in girls, and no self-respecting girl she knew would ever think of dating Wayne Murphy.

So why did she feel good at the thought that she would soon be seeing him again, and of all things, that she would be going with him to Bike Day?

When Wayne arrived home he saw that his brother was still working in the garage. His brother Lynn was twenty-six years old and had been working seven years for the city as a garbage collector. He drove a truck through alleys and dumped the plastic bags left at the alley by residents into the rear of the truck. He supervised three other men, after being promoted in the past year to crew chief.

Lynn was six feet four inches and 240 pounds, a weight-lifter who took great pride in his strength. His muscles were toned as hard as a levee-supporting bag of sand. His father had once muttered to his wife about Lynn having all the muscles in the family and Wayne all the brains. But his wife, speaking as a mother who knew her sons, said both boys had something more than that.

"What?" the father asked.

"They both have good hearts," she said.

As for the boys, never any sibling jealousy. Lynn had recognized at an early age the mental superiority of Wayne, and manifested a kind of awed recognition that shaped itself into a steady pride in his brother's academic achievements. Thus, without any sense of inferiority, Lynn was able to live vicariously through his brother. On his part, Wayne had long appreciated his brother's unusual physical ability, and many times had longed for a similar physique. In Wayne's growing up years, Lynn had sometimes stepped in to render inoperative the attempted intimidation of Wayne by a larger, stronger playpal who sought to exert himself as a bully.

The parents were heartened that Lynn had graduated successfully from high school, and that he had landed a steady, secure job with the city. Benefits and fringes were good, and the outside, physical aspect of his work suited Lynn's own desires and capability. His great hobby, other than weight-lifting, was his working on motorcycles. He always had one or two old bikes in the garage, refurbishing them until they had strong appeal to collectors. This brought him extra income which he quickly converted into more bikes and equipment, which included at present a Honda Goldwing and a Honda CR500R for motocross racing.

Wayne often wondered when Lynn would get a place of his own, but he had built an upstairs apartment over the garage, and seemed as content to live there as a robin in her new spring nest.

"What happened to your face?" Lynn said as soon as he saw Wayne.

"A slight accident," Wayne said.

Lynn looked closely at him. "An accident with a fist?"

"What makes you think that?"

Lynn shook his head. "I've been in too many fights not to recognize the difference between what comes from a doorjamb and an overhand right."

"This came from an uppercut."

Lynn touched his face.

"Awoh!" Wayne exclaimed.

"He didn't connect good on your jaw—more on the side. You'll have a shiner."

"I'll be okay," Wayne said.

"Who did this?" Lynn asked.

"Never mind."

"Who did it?" Lynn asked again.

"Howie," Wayne reluctantly answered.

"Renfro?" Lynn asked thoughtfully. "He's almost twice as big as you. Maybe he ought to be taught to pick on someone his own size."

"No," Wayne said, "this isn't your fight."

"Maybe on Bike Day a couple of the guys and I will have a chance to explain a few things to Howie in a way he can understand."

"I don't need that kind of help," Wayne said. "But there is a way you can help me."

"How's that?"

"Let me ride your bike in the open moto-cross race."

"Hey," he objected, "I was planning to bring home the trophy this year."

"I know, but let me have a go at it."

"Uh-huh—you want to go against Howie? He'll be tough to beat. Cal Withers has been tuning up his Kawasaki. He'll be riding hot iron."

"Hotter than your Honda?"

Lynn grinned. "Maybe not that hot. But Howie is good."

"I want to see how good he is."

Lynn shook his head. "Howie will eat you alive."

Wayne shook his head. "I don't think he'll be able to catch me."

"Wayne, you've got to run that course every day between now and the race. You've got to be familiar with every twist and turn and bump on the course."

"You just make sure the Honda is ready," Wayne said. "I'll be ready."

Lynn shook his head. "Man, you're crazy."

"One other thing," Wayne said.

"Say on," Lynn said.

"I'm taking a girl with me, so I'd like to use your Goldwing."

"And you want me to drive the pickup and tow the CR."

The Goldwing took to the highway as smoothly as a bar of soap on glazed ice. One of the intriguing aspects of biking was how two machines—both two-wheel terrain vehicles—could have so vivid a contrasting personality from each other as did the Goldwing and the CR500R. On the highway the Goldwing was a contented cat, willing to purr comfortably mile after effortless mile. The CR500R was a snarling cub of a mountain lion, growling furiously over every rise and bump that dared challenge its passage. But on this ride the Goldwing's contentment was more than matched by his own, as Wayne was keenly aware of the light pressure of Dawn's arms circling his body. Crawfordville was a small town situated near a TVA-made lake that was a magnet to avid fish anglers in this section of the state, nestled in the foothills leading up to the Lakeland Plateau.

The base camp for the bikers was on the lakeshore located about two miles from town.

Wayne pulled off the highway into the general commotion of arriving bikers, looking for his brother's rig. He passed many Kawasaki bikes, easily recognizable for always being green, and the always white Yamaha bikes. And, of course, he couldn't miss the distinctively red Honda bikes. The con-

trasting colors made it easier for the audience to follow the action of the races.

He spotted Lynn parked near the lake. He pulled
up and introduced Dawn to his brother. He could see
that Lynn was properly impressed.

"Any sign of you know who?" Wayne asked.

Lynn shook his head.

"Who's you know who?" Dawn asked.

"Howie," Wayne said. "I'm going to race against
him in the moto-cross."

She looked disturbed. "I don't want you doing
that."

Her reaction troubled him. "Come here, let's talk."
He led her away to a tree near the water where they
were separate from anyone else. "He handled me
pretty good after we left Barkey's. I don't want to
fight him, but I think I can teach him something if I
can peel his orange in this race."

She frowned. "You don't have to do this."

He grinned. "I may not have to, but I'll feel better
after coming in ahead of him. I don't care about winning, but just making him ride in my dust."

"But how will he feel?"

He shrugged. "Am I supposed to be concerned
about that?"

"No," she said, "maybe not." She was staring at
him and all of a sudden he felt like he stood poised
on a narrow ledge that crossed a chasm of unknown
depth. If he were riding a horse he would be yanking
back on the reins.

"I'm sorry," he said. "What am I missing here?"

She looked away from him then, out over the water. "He's been talking about winning that trophy for
months."

He had no idea of where this was heading, so he waited.

"What Howie and I had is over. It had to end sometime. I always knew that. Now's the time." She turned back to him.

"You're heavy into psychology," she said. "How important do you think his motorcycle is to him?"

"Pretty important," Wayne said.

"He's got two things in his life that he talks about more than anything else. His street bike and his moto-cross bike."

"Okay," Wayne said, "I hear you. You're concerned about his feelings. But what did you think when I asked you to come with me to Bike Day? You knew that Howie and I would see each other, and that he would see you with me. That won't be easy on his feelings."

"Of course I knew he wouldn't like that. But this will make it more clear to him that things aren't the same as they were. But I still like him, and we had a lot of good times together. When he sees me with you, and finds out you're racing against him, he may think I've turned totally against him." Wayne felt like the bitter taste of a bike's exhaust assailed his throat. She said she still liked Howie. But what if her feelings were deeper than that?

She lightly touched his arm. "Howie's not about to win me back," she said. "So the most important thing to him now is to do well in this race."

Wayne turned away. "If I don't race, he probably still won't win. There are some tough riders in the race."

"At least he won't be haunted by who came in ahead of him."

Finally Wayne said, "I still want to race against him."

"I understand," she said. "You do what you want to. It's just . . ." her voice trailed off.

"Just what?" Wayne asked.

She spoke softly. "I understand why you want to beat him, why you want to get even. And I understand how Howie might have been jealous of you, and acted as he did. I don't like what he did, and his actions toward you was one clear reason to change our relationship. But I wish that people could relate to each other not on the basis of winning or losing, or of getting even, but simply on the basis of understanding the feelings of each other and a desire to be kind and supportive and of those feelings."

Wayne checked his protective gear before throwing his leg over his brother's red bike. He glanced around at the other riders—Howie on his green Kawasaki, and six more, each gunning his motor and poised to burst forward over a murderous obstacle-laced course that meandered more than a quarter of a mile before coming back to the starting point.

Wayne's mind was racing faster than his motor. What had Dawn really been saying to him? That deep down she still liked Howie and didn't want to see him hurt more? Wayne felt she was saying more than that. He thought back over her words. She had made clear that the old relationship to Howie was over, but what else was she saying? That she wished people could relate in a different way from any idea of winning or losing or getting even. So now she was leaving Howie behind and looking—for what? Would she be looking for a guy who acted different from Howie, who operated with a different set of values, who would be more caring and considerate of other people's feelings?

The race began, and the roar of the motors echoed behind a mad, bursting scramble of colors as bikes hit the first hill. Wayne saw Howie flash ahead and then the hill was upon him and he felt the sudden lift as he was airborne in a momentary illusion of freedom and then in jarring impact as he moved amid the digging fury of massed bikes as tires pulled against loose dirt. Another hill and then a sharp turn as Wayne accelerated over the mounded risers that jarred him up and down like a yo-yo gone mad. On his next turn he briefly touched his foot down and then he was on his next circuit. He whipped his bike to the left, barely missing a white Yamaha that almost lost it on the turn.

Wayne settled into the race, relishing the thrill of all-out speed that combined with acrobatics to make this a unique event in racing. Four bikes were out of the race by the time Wayne entered the last circuit. He saw Howie just ahead of him, running in third place. They were coming to the last hill before the final turn. This jump required a twisting turn of the wheel in mid-air to position the front wheel in line for the final sprint to the finish line. He was gaining on Howie on the inside as he took the hill. And then Wayne was in the air and twisting. Then he crashed down on the loose dirt and his tires spun crazily, trying to find traction. Then the bike was skidding with Wayne on the ground and his one thought was, I could have beat him.

He wasn't hurt, and was brushing himself off as his brother approached him. "What happened?"

"The brakes must have locked," Wayne said.

Lynn looked at him strangely. "The brakes locked

in mid-air on that last jump? Sure they did." The bike had been perfect, and Wayne knew he'd have more explaining to do later.

"Are you sure you're okay?" The worry in Dawn's voice lifted his heart. Just then Howie appeared. He was grinning. "Too bad about your fall, old buddy. You ran a good race, but there was no way you were going to beat me."

"I'm sorry you didn't win," Wayne said.

Howie looked surprised. "A third-place trophy isn't bad. Next year will be different."

Wayne held out his hand. "I hope you win it next year."

Howie stared at Wayne's hand, and then hesitantly took hold of it.

"I'm glad you weren't hurt."

Wayne nodded. "Thanks." Howie looked at Dawn as though about to say something, then he walked slowly away without looking back.

Wayne and Dawn looked at each other and Wayne shrugged, "Well, Howie beat me."

Her face slowly molded into a huge smile, and he felt her hand slip into his. When he returned the warm pressure he had a sudden insight that he would always remember this day—the day he had lost a race, and won.

WALK STRAIGHT,
WALK FAR

*I met Mrs. Virginia Hoffer because of her in-
volvement with the prison ministry of the Elm
Street Methodist Church. She led this effort at
helping rehabilitate former prisoners who were
trying to adjust to society after years of incar-
ceration. Her effort began with visits to the
prison before inmates were scheduled for release. She organized meetings that dealt with
some area of concern prisoners might have during their time of readjustment. This kind of program is rather unusual for a local church, and
I felt one or more articles might be developed
from the work of Mrs. Hoffer. I met her and
some of the ex-convicts she was helping. One of
these was a man in his early twenties, and after
learning more about Keith Seymour, I discovered another miracle story.*

The prison chaplain talked to him first, coming to
his cell. "Well, Keith," he said. "today's the day."

"That's right, Chaplain."

"Call me Kirk, now that you're going to be a free man."

"All right—Kirk."

Kirk would always be "Chaplain" to Keith. From the very first Chaplain Burnett had reached out to him. Danny Bowen had laughed at him behind his back, but Keith had seen something in the chaplain's thin, almost gaunt face that spoke of a deeper interest in the prisoners than simply the desire to mouth platitudes. The chaplain showed a real empathy for the prisoners and concern for their welfare.

Keith had argued with Danny about the chaplain. Danny had said the chaplain was like everyone else around here—concerned only to maintain order and reach out to get the next paycheck.

"Keith, do you have a place to stay?" the chaplain asked.

Keith nodded. "With my sister for a while," he said. "And Mrs. Hoffer has gotten me a job in one of her car wash locations."

"She's a fine lady," the chaplain said. "She's helped a lot of the fellows. But some of them have let her down." The chaplain looked sharply at Keith.

"I hope you're not one of those."

"I'll never do that," Keith said. "She's done a lot for me, and I'll never forget it."

The chaplain smiled. "She was impressed with your interest in photography."

"Her bringing in those cameras and the photographer to hold that workshop was the highlight of my stay here."

"I'm glad you had at least one highlight while you were here," the chaplain said.

Keith laughed. "Yeah—it sure beat my time in the hole."

The chaplain nodded. "I always wondered why you had that fight with Pete Brewer. Your record to that point was exemplary. You never explained your side. And Danny didn't say anything that would help you."

"Some things you don't do in this place."

"You mean snitch?" the chaplain asked. "But Pete didn't mind talking and he had two witnesses who backed up his version of the fight."

"His friends," Keith said.

"Danny is your friend. Why didn't he help you?"

"It wouldn't have done him any good to point the finger at anyone, especially Pete."

"I'm sorry you were put in solitary, but Danny's silence didn't help you. Was Danny involved in the fight?"

"Danny is not a big guy," Keith said. "Pete is."

"I was just curious," the chaplain said.

"Danny's okay," Keith said. "We go back a long way."

"If you hadn't hurt Pete so severely it wouldn't have gone so bad on you."

"Sometimes, Chaplain, guys have trouble getting the message."

The chaplain held out his hand. "Whatever the message was, I'm sure Pete got it. You've been a good prisoner, Keith, and I wish you good luck on the outside, and hope you never have to come back here. Remember, it's important that you walk straight when you get out of here, but not for just a day, not a short walk. You've got a lifetime ahead of you. So walk straight and walk far."

Keith smiled. "Don't worry, Chaplain, I won't be back."

After Keith put on his civilian clothes, a guard led him down a hallway.

"Where are we going?" Keith asked.

"The warden wants to see you in his office."

The first person Keith saw was a woman in her mid-sixties sitting by the window and holding a package.

"Hello, Mrs. Hoffer," Keith said, surprised.

She smiled at him. "Hello, Keith."

Then the warden cleared his throat. "Well, Keith— the big day is here."

Keith nodded. "Yes, sir."

"Mrs. Hoffer wanted to see you before you left." He gestured toward a chair. "Sit down, Keith."

Keith complied, a little uneasy.

The warden, an overweight man in his late forties with rounded cheeks, always cleared his throat whenever he began talking. Now he lit a big cigar and inhaled deeply to get it started.

The smoke left his lips in a funnel that momentarily blurred his face. Keith noticed that the window-unit air conditioner had leaked, and a rusty stain flowed parallel down the edge of the corner like a pointing clue that solved the mystery of the spot on the aged carpet beneath the window.

"Mrs. Hoffer means a lot to this prison, and she's helped a lot of inmates. I understand she's given you a job in one of her car wash locations."

"That's right," Keith said, glancing at Mrs. Hoffer.

"It's hard for cons to find a job when they get out. You're lucky Mrs. Hoffer is willing to help you."

"I know that," Keith said.

"Mrs. Hoffer wanted to be here for your final in-

terview," the warden said. "She has something she
wants to give you."

"Thank you, Warden," she said, standing and moving to Keith, holding out the package.

Keith fumbled it open, and then caught his breath.
A camera, thirty-five-millimeter Minolta with a full
complement of lenses. He didn't know what to say.

"That's for you," she said, "as a hope for the future. I know you were fascinated by photography
when we offered that workshop. I hope you learn to
be a good photographer. And maybe someday you'll
be able to make a living that way. You might want to
take night courses in photography at Metro Tech
while you're working at the car wash. The important
thing is that you discover what you want to do, and
take the steps needed to reach that goal." She smiled
broadly at him. "And I want to help you in every
way I can."

"Thank you, Mrs. Hoffer," Keith said, visibly
moved.

"I have to get back to town," she said. "May I take
you somewhere?"

Keith shook his head. "Danny is coming after me."

"I try to have my 'boys,' if you don't mind me
calling you that, come to the house once a month to
socialize and talk about any problems. So I'll be in
touch. I don't want to lose contact." She held out her
hand and Keith shook it. She left and the warden said
softly, "That's a great lady. Looks like a sweet old
lady but she has a sharp business mind. Her husband
left her with a lot of businesses to oversee and she
doesn't miss a trick."

"Why is she interested in helping us?"

"Has to do with her son, I reckon. He used to be

in here. Got hooked on drugs in high school and ended up dealing them. He got killed in here."

"I think she's the nicest woman I've ever known," Keith said.

The warden laughed. "She's almost like a guardian angel, but she can't protect you and make everything work out for you on the outside. You're responsible for yourself, and if you get in trouble again she can't keep you from landing back in here—" the warden laughed again, "—in hell."

He flicked ash on the carpet. "She seems to have taken an unusual interest in you," the warden went on. "I don't have to tell you the rules. Don't miss any report to your parole officer. If you leave the city be sure and let him know your schedule, and always make sure he knows where you're living."

"Yes, sir."

The warden stood and held out his hand. "Good luck, then." He pressed a button and a guard appeared.

"You've only given us one hard time. And knowing Pete Brewer I figure that wasn't all your fault. But rules have to be applied here, just as they are applied on the outside. Follow the rules, and you'll be all right."

"Thank you, Warden."

Keith followed the guard out.

When he walked through the front gate he saw Danny parked a half-block away on the other side of the street. At first Keith stood motionless, waiting for the guard's whistle. Then he looked behind him and saw the gate shut. He was free! The full meaning of that did not sink in until he saw a pigeon flutter down to the street twenty feet away. It took three steps and then flew away. Free as a bird! He waved at Danny and began to run toward the car. Danny was grinning and began backing up the car.

They slapped hands as Keith jumped into the car.

"Whose car is this?" Keith asked.

"Mine."

"You're kidding. What'd you do, steal it?"

"Hey, no!" Danny laughed. "We're going straight, remember?"

"*I'm* going straight, at least," Keith said after a moment. "Seriously, how did you get this car?"

"With money I earned."

Keith scoffed. "Yeah, sure—you saved enough from your job at the car wash."

They rode in silence a few moments, and Danny glanced at Keith and quickly looked away.

Keith sighed. "Okay, let's have it. What's the story?"

"I earned the money at the car wash."

"This is me," Keith said, "the guy who's known you all your life. The guy who was stupid enough to go with you and break into that jewelry store. The guy who got arrested with you and sent to the slammer with you. You can't lie to me."

"Okay, but the thing is, I really did earn the money at the car wash. Your brother-in-law has rigged up a sweet little deal."

"What are you talking about?"

"A way to get cars at almost no risk."

"If Ernie's involved there's plenty of risk."

"No, no," Danny said, "he's an all right guy."

"He's a jar of pond scum."

"Wait till you hear. I know he'll cut you in. It works this way," Danny explained. "A guy drives his car to the car wash. I ask the guy what service he wants; he tells me and I mark a slip of paper and give it to him to take to the cashier and pay.

"But if the car is a particular model that George wants—"

"Who's George?" Keith asked.

"He's a good friend of Ernie. He runs the chop shop."

"I don't like any of this," Keith said.

"Wait till you hear the rest. Anyway, here's this car, maybe a late model, maybe an older model that's popular. The driver hands me his key so I can take the car to the start of the car wash."

"So?"

"I make an impression of the key."

"And you're going to use the key you make to steal the car."

"Right!" Danny exclaimed.

"A couple of problems," Keith said. "You don't know where the guy lives."

"This is where it's a little chancy," Danny admitted. "I put my initial in one corner of the slip of paper the guy hands the cashier. At the end of the day when she's checking her cash against receipts, she notices my initial that this is the car where I want an address, and she sees if the guy paid by check. Most people pay by check, and the addresses are printed on the checks."

"And if the guy pays cash—no luck?"

Danny shrugged. "We can't win them all. But if it pans out, we have a key and an address. We can check out the place at all hours, and move in on the car without any risk of having to break in with someone maybe seeing us, or a car alarm going off. It's just like we own the car. Walk up, get it, and drive off. Minimum of fuss and risk."

"So the cashier's in on it?"

Danny nodded. "When she matches the check with the slip I marked, she writes down the address, and we're home free."

"What you're asking for is another visit to a free home you haven't been away from very long."

Danny shook his head. "It's a sweet setup. We deliver the cars to George, he pays Ernie, and Ernie splits with us."

"I thought you learned enough about Ernie last time."

"This is different. Ernie is sorry about last time. He thought he had fixed the alarm."

"He cased the place, told us he had it all worked out. Told us exactly what to do, not to worry about any alarm. We trusted him, except he didn't know about the second alarm, and we're the ones who got caught and sent to prison.

"He really appreciates us not squealing on him. Says he never worried; he knew all the time we weren't snitches. Says he wants to take care of us now, to make it up to us."

"Did he ask you to spread all this out to me?"

Danny nodded. "He said he wasn't sure how you were feeling about him. Said you weren't too friendly the last time he saw you."

Keith laughed. "You mean when I decked him the day before we were shipped out? If my sister hadn't been standing there I might have put him in the hospital."

"Yeah, well—he wants everything to be better now."

"Look," Keith said, "I've never liked him. I didn't want my sister to marry him, but she did and she still seems to love him. She'd crack up if she knew he were involved in ripping off cars."

Keith mused. "She pretty much raised me after Mother died. She was the big reason I kept Ernie's name away from the cops after the jewelry store fiasco." He shook his head. "I'll be glad when I can find another place to stay. I hate having to be polite to him in front of Ruth."

"Are you in on the deal?" Danny asked.

Keith looked at Danny and laughed.

"No way."

The house was in an area halfway between downtown and the Britton Green subdivision. Most of the houses were built in the 1930s and were considered of "historic" interest by residents, but the real historic neighborhood, with houses from the 1920s and earlier, was a few blocks further toward Britton Green. These older houses were in demand and commanded high prices, but his sister's house was the nicest she ever had lived in. Wooden, painted green, with a screened-in side porch. Very homey and solid-looking, like a house built to last.

Danny stopped in front.

"I'll be by for you at eight in the morning," Danny said. Keith waved as Danny pulled away.

Keith walked up the aggregate sidewalk toward the house when the front door opened and Ruth appeared with open arms. Keith rushed forward and they collided with a hug.

Keith felt the sharp sting of tears. She had been his protector growing up. Now he was her protector, even if she didn't realize it. She had married a good-looking guy who exhibited the goodwill of a pro scout recruiting an All-American senior. That's how he courted Ruth, with an eager earnestness that appeared to hide nothing but hid everything. He had always seemed too nice, too anxious to please, too agreeable. Keith had distrusted him on that basis alone, before he had anything else to consider. He tried once to communicate his reservations to Ruth before the wedding, but with nothing concrete except his feelings, she laughed it off. Ernie was a good man with a good job, driving a truck for Allied Cartage.

But not long after the wedding Ernie came on to Keith with his patented eager boy-let's-be-friends routine. And then one night after a quantity of beers had blurred Keith's mental activity, Ernie had spoken of a guy he knew who could get them lots of easy money. Turns out this guy was a fence who would take merchandise with no questions asked. And Keith, a teenager who had been dirt poor all his life, having no father, and a mother who worked as a cleaning maid at a downtown hotel, fantasized about having a few things that would make life a little more bearable and walked into the biggest mistake he had ever made. And in the process found nothing to alter his original distrust of Ernie.

He would never forget his conversation with Ernie on a day after he was out on bail, and before he was sentenced.

Ernie had asked him to go with him to the Riverfront Park. He had been his usual eager, wanting-to-please self.

"Look, kid," he said, "I'm really sorry. I appreciate your keeping me out of it."

"Thank Ruth," Keith said.

"You didn't tell her anything?"

"No."

"Good," Ernie said, relief in his voice. "I really

mean it. I love Ruth more than anything. And I never want to hurt her."

"Then stop being a crook," Keith said.

Ernie laughed. "That's a thought, stop being a crook. But everybody's a crook. They just don't get arrested. Everybody in this world is trying to figure out how to take money from someone else. Through advertising, or selling something. Or through offering advice about religion or the stock market or what kind of medicine you should take. It all comes down to other people having money and you don't, and the question is what gimmick are you going to use to get some of it for yourself. Going after things in a store or somebody's house is just a simpler, quicker way of getting it. Basically, it's all the same."

"Ruth wouldn't think it was the same."

Ernie winked and smiled. "I plan to be successful in my work. I'll probably be bringing home more than she might expect, but I'm sure she'll be gratified I'm doing so well in my job and able to bring home a bonus from time to time."

"Listen, Ernie," Keith said. "You straighten up your act or I'll tell Ruth all about your part in the robbery. If she learns the truth she'll be talking to a divorce lawyer before the cops have a chance to talk to you."

Ernie stared at him for a moment, and then nodded. "You're right, Keith. You're right. From now on it's strictly the straight and narrow." He held out his hand to Keith. "I'll never forget what you're doing for me, carrying all the load. But I'll make it up to you."

Keith took Ernie's hand and knew that he would need something to hold on to during the next few years, but this hand wasn't it.

Now, holding Ruth, he thought about what he had to do and how he would do it. His covenant to keep quiet about Ernie was dependent on Ernie's staying straight. According to Danny, Ernie was hip deep in mud. That meant no more protecting Ruth from the truth. But first, he needed to talk to Ernie and hear what he had to say.

Dinner that night was Keith's favorite, flank steak covered with onions. Ruth excelled with this meal. If Ruth noticed any strain between Keith and Ernie she did not let on. Her manner was upbeat throughout, urging Keith to eat more.

After the meal Keith said, "Ernie and I are going to take a little walk." A quick frown passed over Ruth's face, and Keith smiled. "We're going to get caught up on some things. Won't be gone long."

Outside Keith said, "Let's walk down to Baylor's." Baylor's was a convenience store located four blocks away.

As they were walking Keith said, "Danny told me an interesting story."

"What'd you think?" Ernie asked.

Keith turned on him and stopped walking. "What did you think I thought? I just got out of the dog pound. You think I want to go back?"

"This scam is foolproof. No one's going to get caught."

"You broke our agreement," Keith said. "The straight and narrow, you promised. And I'd say nothing to Ruth. Now she's going to learn what she married."

Ernie reached his hand into his pocket.

"What have you got there?" Keith asked.

"You don't want to know."

Keith grinned. "A gun? You have a gun? Shooting me will really endear you to Ruth."

"Muggings aren't unusual in this neighborhood."

"A good plan, Ernie. I get shot by the mugger and you get rid of an unregistered gun and who's to know the difference? The only problem is the cops won't buy it."

"They'll find out you're an ex-con, once thrown into solitary after a bad fight in prison. They'll believe you resisted the mugger and got shot."

"And there's no one who will contradict your story?"

Ernie grinned. "Do you see someone who will?"

Keith was looking past Ernie's left shoulder. "Only that old woman walking her dog."

Ernie glanced quickly behind him and Keith dove forward, crashing against Ernie's knees. Ernie grunted and fell backward, struggling to get his gun out of his pocket. He hit hard on his back and the gun flew out of his hand. Ernie's foot lashed out and caught Keith's jaw and Keith fell on his side. He reached out and grabbed Ernie's other ankle and pulled hard. He hammered his fist into Ernie's nose and felt the cartilage go. Blood poured down Ernie's face, and Keith felt it spreading over his hands as he clutched Ernie's throat. They rolled over and over on the ground and Keith felt the gun as his back made contact. Suddenly Ernie grunted as he found the gun and pulled the gun toward Keith's head.

"Too bad, Keith," Ernie gasped as Keith grabbed his wrist with both hands. They continued rolling, Ernie's hand with the gun squeezed between their bodies. The shot was muffled. Keith felt nothing. His one regret was that Ruth would never know the truth.

Ernie quit struggling, and suddenly Keith was on

top. Ernie was groaning, his head shifting back and forth. Keith took the gun from his hand, and then looked closer. He winced at what he saw. There was new blood now, on Ernie's pants four inches below his belt buckle.

Keith slapped Ernie's face. "Ernie—Ernie, listen to me. You're not going to die. But I think you can kiss fatherhood good-bye."

The whole thing was a mess. The ambulance taking Ernie to the hospital. And then the explanations. The cops took Keith over it again and again. They didn't buy the reason for the fight. "He didn't want you to tell his wife the truth about his involvement with a car-theft ring? Let's go over it again. Take us through what happens at the car wash again."

And on and on until Keith felt his tongue could apply for disability insurance.

Ruth couldn't believe it. Eventually she had to accept it. But Keith could see in her eyes that she still loved Ernie.

Danny admitted his role in the car thefts, and for giving evidence was promised a more lenient charge in his forthcoming trial. As for himself, Keith was asked by Mrs. Hoffer to come to her house. He had taken a cab to the entrance and had walked the rest of the way up the long winding driveway. He carried his Minolta camera, wishing he could take some shots of the spacious grounds. He rang the doorbell, and nervously fingered his camera. She opened the door for him and invited him to enter.

She led him to a sitting room where he sat in a chair that supported him with the softness of a cloud.

She smiled. "Well, young man, I've helped other prisoners who have gotten into trouble after getting out, but you've set a record for being the fastest. The police have given me some details, but I wanted to hear it from you. I'm particularly interested in the way my car wash is being used to facilitate the theft of cars."

So Keith went over it again. She probed him further about his relationship with his brother-in-law, going back to Keith's first arrest.

Finally, she nodded. "A most unusual story," she said. "It seems to me that almost everything you did after your first arrest was not done for your self-interest. You wanted to protect the feelings of your sister, you wanted her husband to straighten himself out, and then you realized the time had come to tell your sister the truth."

"I'd give anything if I hadn't been involved in that robbery attempt at the store."

"And you've paid your debt to society for that mistake. People make mistakes, particularly when they are as young as you were. The important thing is not only that people pay for their mistakes, but that they recognize they were wrong and determine to make changes in their life. I believe this is what the criminal justice system should try to accomplish and why I try to help all I can."

Keith spoke slowly. "The warden told me about your son, Mrs. Hoffer. I'm sorry."

"He made his mistake, and he paid for it. Every time I see someone come out and go straight, I think of him and wish he could have had the same chance." She smiled and added, "I have high hopes for you, Keith."

"I'll make it," he said, "and a lot of credit will go to you. Your giving me a job will let me keep going while I go to night school and study photography, like you suggested."

"I see you brought your camera with you today."

"I hope you don't mind, but—" he hesitated, "—I wanted to take some pictures of you that I can keep." He grinned. "Someday when I'm good, I hope I can take a real picture of you with the right shadowing, kind of like those pictures you see of Winston Churchill and other famous people, that captures their personality."

She smiled. "I'm glad you want to go to school and study photography, but maybe the best way to learn is to learn on the job."

Keith stared at her questioningly.

"My husband dabbled in a lot of things. He collected businesses like some people collect coins. One of the businesses he got into was photography. Did you ever hear of Olin Myer's Studios?"

"No."

"They specialize in portraiture. I've talked to Olin about you. He could use another assistant. You'd be learning darkroom work as well as cameras and lighting. Are you interested?"

Keith felt like he was unglued from the planet, somewhere floating and waiting for reality to hit. All he wanted was an opportunity, and it looked like he was not only being given the chance to walk straight, but walk far.

He wanted to hug Mrs. Hoffer, hold her close and tell her how he felt about her. But although he was a free man, he knew he wasn't free to do that yet.

But he'd be working on it.